# The Shires of York

## One: The Age of Darkness

## by

## Joseph Murphy-James

# Copyright

Copyright © 2017 by Wise Grey Owl Limited

All rights reserved. This book or any portion thereof may not be reproduced or used in any manner whatsoever without the express written permission of the publisher except for the use of brief quotations in a book review.

Published in the United Kingdom of Great Britain & Northern Ireland and subject to the Laws of England and Wales.

First Published, 2017

ISBN 9781520900629

Published by Wise Grey Owl Limited

www.wisegreyowl.co.uk

www.wisegrayowl.com

# Dedication

2015 saw the death of Sir Terry Pratchett, an inspirational writer who saw clearly the absurdities of western culture and was able to take logic to its extremes in a humorous and intelligent way.

I was researching this book when Terry died and he has influenced its direction posthumously.

"HE IS HAPPY ABOUT THAT."

# Key Characters

**Dämonen**

Lord Alaric, Lord of Dämonen

Albert, High Priest

Bjarke, Doorman

Eburwin, High Priest

Gervas, High Priest

Baron von Brunhild

Arnaude, Alder

Diabolus, the Devil

Tanja

**Humans**

Venutius, King of Brigantes, Previous mate of Queen

Vellocatus, Mate of Queen, Prior Armour bearer of Venutius

Cartimandua, Queen of Brigantes

Godric, Merchant, ally of Cartimandua

Eoforwine and Wilfrid, horsemen

Justus, 2nd in command to Venutius

Ramm, Anglo Saxon warrior

Virgil, Anglo Saxon warrior, Ramm's 2nd in command

Leng, Merchant

Rice, Merchant

# Key Characters

**Elven**

Tanyl, M, Council of Two

Ioelena, F, Council of Two

Llarm, M, Quorum (8) Council, elder Elf

Alanys, F, Quorum Council, young Elf

Elidir, M, Quorum Council, Elf of some standing

Harik, M, Quorum Council, warrior Elf

Elorø, F, Quorum Council, elder Elf

Avae, F Score (20) Council, Healer

Quinn, M Score Council, Warrior

**Dragons**

Tanwen, Fire Manon

Padrig, Mate of Tanwen

Buddug, Daughter

Dona, Daughter

Delyth, Padrig's old flame

# Chapter 1: Fend for Yourselves

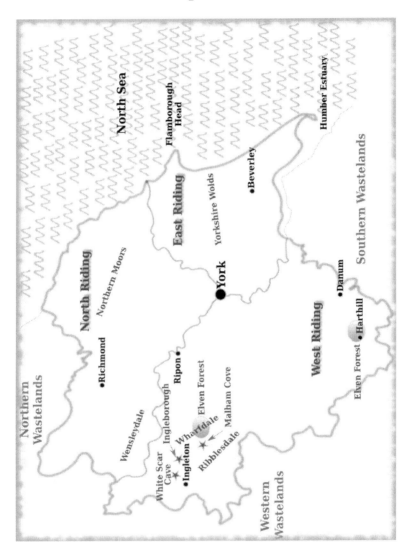

# 1 – Fend for Yourselves

"The affairs of man are not of my concern," said Lord Alaric.

"They will impact The Veils," said the demon Albert and he sniffed.

It was a habit of the High Priest and it further irritated the tetchy Alaric.

"Stop sniffing," he snapped and the air sparkled from his power.

Albert stepped back, crestfallen but not beaten. He blew his nose, depositing voluminous quantities of mucus into a piece of dirty cloth, which he placed back into his cape pocket. Alaric gave him a look of disgust; that was easy for Lord Alaric.

"It is the Queen herself that has requested your assistance," said Albert.

"Ah," said Alaric, "Queen she may think she is but, in the scheme of things, she is of nothing and certainly not to me."

Albert rolled his eyes and flapped his wings gently. This was going to add further difficulty to a morning that had been a trial caused by his cohorts, the other priests.

"She says that she has news of the whereabouts of the number three," Albert added, stifling a sniff, causing his speech

# Chapter 1: Fend for Yourselves

to take on a nasal tone.

He had the Lord's attention.

"The third Crystal of The Veils," Albert added.

"The third," said Alaric, "and the second too?"

Lord Alaric raised his scaly hands and pointed a claw at the High Priest, who took a step backward. Alaric moved towards Albert and the Lord's tail scraped noisily on the stone floor of the great hall.

"Not the second, Lord, just the third," Albert said, holding his ground as the Lord advanced. Alaric no longer intimidated Albert.

Alaric stopped and he turned his head slightly, stretching his wings at the same time. The devil's horns on his head glowed and Alaric's power was evident.

"We have the first already," mused Alaric, "and the third would be a good addition but we will need the second to allow us to complete the first Veil. Is that not true, High Priest?"

"Indeed, Lord," said Albert.

"You know this for sure? She knows the whereabouts of the third crystal?" asked Alaric.

"In as much as one can trust mankind," replied Albert.

"Yes," said Alaric, "tell Cartimandua, so called Queen of the Brigantes, that Lord Alaric, High Priest Albert and Baron von

# Chapter 1: Fend for Yourselves

Brunhild will commune with her after the next full moon. The usual show of force too; you understand, I am sure."

"Thank you Lord," said Albert, sniffing.

He gave a low bow, bringing his tail between his legs, lowered his wings and backed towards the twin wooden doors of the great hall. Lord Alaric remained standing, stretched his wings, pushed his tail out to one side and raised his head. These were the rituals of power of the Dämonen.

Albert sneezed loudly after he'd shut the doors firmly behind him. He stood on a ledge with a sheer drop to jagged rocks below. The great hall of Lord Alaric was the top peak of the Land of the Dämonen, built into the fabric of the mountain. Other quarters were constructed in the lesser peaks; the High Priests' accommodation was only slightly below that of the Lord's residence. From casual observation the Land of Dämonen was a mountain range; the workings within were obscured and out of bounds to all, except the Dämonen, or so they thought.

High Priest Albert stretched his muscular wings and flapped them vigorously. He threw himself from the platform outside the door of the great hall and swooped down to the peak below, landing proficiently on a ledge. He folded his wings, raised his scaled and clawed hand and mouthed the spell that would cast

# Chapter 1: Fend for Yourselves

back the stone that blocked the entrance to the Kapell, the home of the High Priests.

Behind the stone door stood Bjarke, the doorman, general dogs body and butler. He was a devil, like Albert, but tall and stocky in stature, ugly in appearance, lacking in intelligence of any kind but as loyal as a dog.

"Master," he said and bowed his head. Being deformed, having no tail, nor wings it was the best he could do and, to Albert, it was an acceptable gesture.

Albert lifted his tail clear of the floor and swept into the Kapell. Bjarke took Albert's cloak, as he had done many times, and Albert made his way to the altar room. He knew that the other High Priests would be waiting for news of his audience with Lord Alaric. Albert was one of three High Priests but was prime among equals and only Albert was granted an audience with the Lord.

*A mixed blessing.*

Albert entered the room to be greeted by High Priests Eburwin and Gervas who bowed, their tails between their legs and wings folded. Albert extended his wings and swished his tail to one side in a return gesture.

*They are impatient for news.*

"Well?" said Gervas.

## Chapter 1: Fend for Yourselves

"He will see her," said Albert to expectant faces, "and he wants von Brunhild too and the usual show of our power."

"To be expected," said Eburwin.

"The crystal, will we recover it?" said High Priest Gervas.

"That's what this is about," said Albert, "without that likely outcome, he would not have bitten, for sure."

Albert sniffed.

"When?" said Eburwin.

"The next moon, Eburwin, a few weeks time. We have much to arrange," said Albert.

Gervas nodded.

"Gervas, can you spare a messenger, a trusted one who can cross into the Shires of York? We need to inform the Queen. She will come, I am sure, but she will need to travel. Today, can we message the Queen today?"

"It will be done," said Gervas and he ruffled his wings in anticipation, "I have an Alder bird available and I would trust her with my life."

*An Alder. Vicious things but tenacious and their spirit is able to leave Dämonen. A good choice.*

"Do it now please, Gervas. Time within the Shires is our enemy," said Albert and he sniffed again.

Gervas left through an arched exit carved into the stone wall;

## Chapter 1: Fend for Yourselves

Albert and Eburwin were alone. Eburwin was a competent High Priest of long standing, probably a millennium; nobody knew. Albert was a relative newcomer having served a mere five hundred years or so, whilst Gervas tenure was nearly six hundred. Their apprenticeships had been long and arduous in the Priesthood of Dämonen, the ruling caste of the Shires. Their role was nothing less than the smooth operation of all aspects of life within the land of the Shires of York; this included dominion over all lifeforms that inhabited the Shires. Many of them did not know this and had to be reminded.

"There is talk of withdrawal of the Romans," said Eburwin as Gervas left.

"Ah, mankind, yes," replied Albert, "I had heard. That will leave Queen Cartimandua exposed. She relies on their support. King Venutius will take advantage of her weakness. He has not forgiven her."

"The dealings of man. They are such a cantankerous species," mused Eburwin, "they seem not to know that they are being tested."

"Stupid, for sure, and they squander their short life force on their power struggles. You know of Venutius, Eburwin?"

"A little, Albert. Were the Queen and he not mated and she severed their relationship. The warrior Vellocatus replaced him,

# Chapter 1: Fend for Yourselves

I believe. Previously, he was a servant of King Venutius; their egos are easily bruised."

"Yes, Eburwin, Venutius has tried to oust the Queen on a few occasions but the Queen has always had the protection of Rome, until now. But, these issues are little concern of ours; the Crystals of the Veils are the only things that interest us. It appears that the Queen has some knowledge, or she is playing a very dangerous game."

"As we may be doing," said Eburwin, "if she proves to be lying."

"She tells the truth," said Albert, and he sniffed, "of that I am sure. It is the price she wishes to extract that is my concern and whether Lord Alaric will pay it."

"You mean?" said Eburwin.

"The affairs of mankind, Eburwin. She will want us involved. He will not countenance that."

"He may have to," said Gervas as he re-entered the chamber.

"Lord Alaric is not predisposed to having to do anything," said Eburwin, raising his claw towards Gervas, "he will set the terms."

"That, he will," said Albert, "but arguing between ourselves will solve nothing. The stage is set and it is now for the actors to perform. May they perform well."

# Chapter 1: Fend for Yourselves

"The Alder is on its way," said Gervas, changing the subject and lightening the mood.

"Who have you sent?" asked Eburwin.

*They are all ill tempered.*

"Arnaude," said Gerard, "she is the swiftest of them and will make haste. She is tenacious and will see that the job is done."

*

Lord Alaric stood by the window in the great hall of Dämonen and looked out, his tail supporting the bulk of his weight.

*It isn't real, of course, none of it. The Shires of York have no mountains.*

This was a fact. Dämonen was a temporal aberration, mountains borrowed from elsewhere and invisible to most of the residents of the Shires, but not to all of them.

Yet, Lord Alaric was the Tacit Ruler of the Shires and nothing much happened without Alaric's involvement. He believed that the Shires would not exist without him. Few of its inhabitants knew this or cared; they should.

He smelt it first; the acrid smell of Hades.

*Unmistakable.*

The fabric of the Shires was rupturing and smoke oozed into the great hall. The floor opened and, through the slot, preceded

# Chapter 1: Fend for Yourselves

by bright bursts of light, slid a wizened creature. He was no taller than a child but his skin was tough and leathery and his devilish head was adorned with two horns that glowed brightly in the dim light of the hall. His wings were extended and his tail outstretched in greeting. He carried a trident.

"Diabolus," said Alaric, "you make such an entrance."

"It is expected," said the newcomer, his voice weak and effeminate.

*Not by me.*

Alaric returned a ritualised welcome; not quite subservient but showing respect to Diabolus.

*He is my superior, after all, nominally.*

"To what do I owe this honour?" asked Alaric.

"The third crystal," whined Diabolus, "I hear that you may know of its whereabouts."

"You are well informed, as always, Diabolus."

*Damn, I was hoping to keep this hidden for a little while longer.*

"The third is not much good without the second," said Diabolus.

"No, I would have preferred to find the second but we must not sniff at the third. After all, it will allow us to create our first Veil."

# Chapter 1: Fend for Yourselves

"Two crystals without the second, is that wise Lord Alaric?"

*The way he looks at me and the way he rubs his hands. What does he really mean? Why does he not say?*

"I am not sure that I understand," said Alaric.

"Oh, but you do, yes, you do. Think Lord, think," said Diabolus and he hissed.

Diabolus, bent and stooped, paced around the great hall to stand by the window. He was not tall enough to look out so he turned to face Alaric and was framed by the light streaming in.

*Such a diminutive figure but I do not underestimate his strength.*

"You will know, in time, you will know. I came to warn you," said Diabolus, "not to meddle."

"Meddle?" said Alaric.

"Meddle with the order of the Crystals of the Veils. The Shires are yours Alaric and I will not interfere. Put my dominions at risk and I will intervene."

*A threat?*

"A promise," said Diabolus, as if reading Lord Alaric's thoughts.

*Riddles, Diabolus loves riddles.*

The smoke cleared and Diabolus slipped back through the floor; he left as quickly as he arrived and the odour of Hades

# Chapter 1: Fend for Yourselves

drifted away with him.

Alaric's mood soured.

*

The spirit of Arnaude, the messenger bird, circled high above the tented area that housed Queen Cartimandua's army outside of the walled city of York.

*She is not there.*

Arnaude's senses were acute; they were seeking the whereabouts of the Queen.

*She is in the City.*

Eboracum, the Roman interlopers had named Lord Alaric's city; he was having no truck and maintained his appointed name of York.

The alder leaned into the wind and descended to the rooftops, scattering small birds and mammals.

*Later, my lovelies, I will eat later and then you will neither hear nor see me.*

Queen Cartimandua was with Vellocatus, her commander and partner. They were discussing something and the atmosphere was tense. Arnaude entered the room through the window, without opening it, and landed with a swishing sound on a chair back.

Vellocatus, startled, drew his sword but his arm became

# Chapter 1: Fend for Yourselves

leaden and he re-sheathed it.

*You have no choice.*

The Queen turned to face Arnaude.

"You are Lord Alaric's messenger. Am I right?"

*I am Arnaude, messenger of Alaric, Lord of Dämonen, creator of the Shires to purvey a message to Cartimandua, Queen of the Brigantes, protected by Rome. You are she.*

The Queen could hear Arnaude's thoughts; the message was for her and her alone. Vellocatus was in the dark.

"I am Queen Cartimandua."

*I must see you alone.*

Cartimandua turned to Vellocatus and said, "You must leave me with the messenger."

Vellocatus paused briefly, bowed and took his leave.

"I will not be far away my liege," said Vellocatus as he left the room.

*I am ready to convey the message. I will relay it once only. Are you ready to receive it Cartimandua, Queen of the Brigantes?*

The Queen looked poised and said, "Yes, I am ready. You may proceed."

*Lord Alaric, through his High Priest Albert, has agreed to consort with you and you will assemble your entourage at the*

# Chapter 1: Fend for Yourselves

*Cove of Malham in the Dales of the Shires of York at noon on the day following the new moon. You are to assemble at the foot of the cove on the east bank of Malham Beck.*

*Lord Alaric expects discourse concerning the third Crystal of The Veils and will be sorely disappointed if none is forthcoming.*

*That is the end of my message to you Cartimandua, Queen of the Brigantes. Do you have a response to relay to Lord Alaric through his High Priest Albert?*

"Thank you Messenger Arnaude. Yes, if you would give me a moment, I would like to compose a reply."

The Queen strolled over to the window and looked out at the bustling streets below; commerce was in motion with its associated grime.

*Momentous things are happening but, for some, life continues as normal.*

"I have this response, if you will, Arnaude," she said, "I am honoured that Lord Alaric has acknowledged my request for an audience. I will be pleased to accept his invitation and the Lord, through his High Priest, can be assured that Queen Cartimandua will be true to her word."

*Is that the end of the message?*

"A little more, please, Arnaude," said the Queen, "If I may

# Chapter 1: Fend for Yourselves

be so bold, may I remind Lord Alaric that there is a bargain to be struck and that I, Cartimandua, Queen of the Brigantes, will be seeking protection from the Dämonen in a binding treaty. Only then can I release the knowledge that I hold."

*I will relay your message to Albert, High Priest of Dämonen.*

The alder raised its wings and circled the room before exiting through the closed window. The room fell silent and Queen Cartimandua was alone.

*

Albert stood before Lord Alaric.

"She seeks my protection, through a treaty with the Dämonen?"

"Yes, Lord," said Albert and he sniffed.

The air buzzed with Alaric's irritation at the suggestion and at Albert's nasal problems.

"Such impertinence," said Alaric, "and unprecedented. Why would I become involved in the petty squabbles of these creatures?"

*Is that a rhetorical question?*

Albert remained silent. Alaric knew the answer.

A glass globe at the centre of a high stone table in the middle of the great hall, rolled to one side and then returned to its original position. Lord Alaric was thinking. He motioned over

# Chapter 1: Fend for Yourselves

to the table and idly picked up the ornament; it dissolved in his hand and reappeared in the other. He repeated it several times whilst he pondered his dilemma.

*These creatures will live their short lives but we will remain and the Veils will be their legacy. What is the harm? The third crystal is the prize but where will a treaty lead us? What will we be forced to do in its name whilst this vile Queen lives?*

"I have decided, High Priest," said Alaric in due course as he replaced the globe on the table.

"Yes?" said Albert.

"You must do more work, Albert, and stop sniffing!" said Alaric.

*He always uses my name, rather than High Priest, when he wants something of me.*

"Yes, Lord?"

"You need to gain this Queen's trust. Communicate with her again and discuss the terms of the treaty. Tell her that I need to know exactly what is expected of us? We cannot be at the beck and call of this Queen. Chapter and verse, you understand?"

*A delaying tactic? A subterfuge?*

"Yes, Lord."

"Do this before we consort with her. That is my decision."

*I'm being dismissed.*

# Chapter 1: Fend for Yourselves

"Yes, Lord," said Albert for there was nothing further to say.

\*

Albert checked first. Queen Cartimandua was at her camp and was alone, except for her servants and guards.

*I need an audience.*

The Queen recognised the voice in her head immediately. This was not new to her. She dismissed her servants and instructed the guard to remain outside but to leave her alone.

"You may have your audience, High Priest of Dämonen," said the Queen to the empty room.

Albert materialised before the Queen into a form acceptable to her eyes; he calculated that the bedevilled reality would have been too much for her to bear. He was wrong, for the Queen was strong of character.

"You have news?" said Queen Cartimandua.

*I have a request from Lord Alaric, creator and ruler of the Shires of York.*

The Queen looked at the representation of Albert standing before her. Humanoid it was, but there was something that wasn't right.

*Too perfect perhaps?*

Albert relayed, suitably framed, Lord Alaric's reservations about the treaty she'd proposed. Her response surprised him.

## Chapter 1: Fend for Yourselves

"As I would have expected, High Priest," she said, "and what will you need from me to curb the disquiet of Lord Alaric?"

*I need to know exactly what you require from the Dämonen. We need to work out the terms of any treaty between us.*

Queen Cartimandua raised her eyebrows. She saw this as a positive step; discussing terms meant that an agreement between them was being taken seriously.

"What does this entail, pray?"

*I will need full details of what you will expect of us. Only a complete picture will satisfy Lord Alaric.*

The Queen paced around the room, deep in thought. Albert's apparition remained still.

Finally, Queen Cartimandua said, "Let us start."

*This may make some time Queen of the Brigantes. You may need to alert your entourage.*

The discussions started and finally ended.

*

"So, the Roman occupiers are leaving, is that what you are saying High Priest?"

"Yes, Lord. Queen Cartimandua has been told specifically that she is to fend for herself. She is no longer under the protection of Rome. Venutius, Nominal King of the Brigantes

# Chapter 1: Fend for Yourselves

and her previous mate, wishes to depose her and will join with the Angles to fight her, once the Roman legions have withdrawn fully."

"Angles, jangles," said Alaric, "I care little for the games that are played by mankind. The Angles, are they not the mercenaries of Rome in any case?"

"Yes, and that puts them in a strong position to take control after Rome."

Alaric sighed.

*It tires me. Let them fight their petty wars. They do not concern me. Only the Veils matter. Ah, the Veils!*

Albert walked a dangerous line by saying, "You are Lord of the Shires. All in the Shires of York are yours; it is your domain."

Alaric snarled, stretched out his wings, and said, "Don't lecture me High Priest. I know my responsibilities; thus has it been for aeons."

"Yes, Lord."

*He understands what must be done for the sake of the Veils.*

"You have the terms of Queen Cartimandua's proposed treaty, Lord. I will take my leave, if you will, so that you may deliberate," said Albert and a smile drifted across his face.

Following the ritualised departure, Albert closed the door of

# Chapter 1: Fend for Yourselves

the great hall, sniffed and then breathed deeply. He stretched out his wings and leapt from the high balcony, flying high into the mountains for pleasure, before returning to his quarters at the Kapell.

*The stage is set. The consequences uncertain.*

*

Alaric opened the door at the rear of the great hall and walked down the steps hewn into the granite. Deep into the mountain he went until he encountered another door of a light blue wood of heavy construction. It had no handle and no obvious way to gain entry.

He waved his claw, muttered an incantation and waited a moment. The door slid upwards, revealing a large cave with a podium at the centre. The cavern was lit by eternal litstones embedded in its walls, each recycling photons of light to give the room a comfortable brightness. The podium was of pale marble with a brightly polished surface.

Alaric entered and walked over to the dais and placed his scaly hands around its edge and the podium responded to Alaric's touch, probing him for identity; it was satisfied. Its surface dissolved, revealing the crystal chamber, the source of the power of the Veils. A deep intricately shaped slot was visible, designed to hold the twelve Crystals of the Veils, one

# Chapter 1: Fend for Yourselves

on top of another. Only one crystal was in place, number one and its intricate shape matched perfectly the pattern of the slot.

*But it is more than that.*

Not only was the niche for each crystal a model for it but the channel through which it passed, when put in place, demanded that each crystal be placed in turn into the crystal chamber.

*The crystal chamber requires that number two be the next one to be placed. We will have number three. What will I do with the crystal while we wait for number two, for it cannot be placed into the chamber?*

Alaric knew that, in the wrong hands, a crystal could be a powerful weapon; the Dämonen had their enemies in the Shires and, until at least one of the Veils was opened, their influence was restricted. The way that they could interact with sentient beings was limited and Alaric could work only within those restraints. The Veils would change all of that.

*I have ruled this land for years. I won my position by conquest and will not relinquish it willingly. Under my watch, the four Veils will be opened. That will be my legacy.*

Alaric removed his hands from the podium and the surface solidified. He turned away from the crystal chamber and left through the only apparent entrance; it closed silently behind him. He ascended the stairs back towards the great hall.

# Chapter 1: Fend for Yourselves

*I know what I have to do.*

*

"Are you sure that you can trust them?" said Vellocatus.

A servant was adjusting his armour and weapons; they were making preparation to travel north west to Malham Cove.

"Do we have a choice?" said the Queen.

"Yes, my liege," said her partner, "we have an army, we can fight Venutius."

"We will lose if we do," she snapped, "he has joined forces with the Angles, our erstwhile colleagues, who now see an opportunity to rule."

"Relying on the Dämonen carries great risks too," said Venutius, "we are of little consequence to them, like ants that can be stamped upon at their whim. Why should they offer us protection?"

"You are right to an extent," said Queen Cartimandua and she turned to face him, brushing her servant aside for a moment, "but they value what we have."

"The crystal. So you say, but it looks of nothing to me."

Cartimandua unwrapped a leather parcel to reveal a piece of rock. It was intricately shaped but, to Vellocatus' eyes, it looked unimpressive.

"Feel its surface, Vellocatus, it pulses with warmth."

# Chapter 1: Fend for Yourselves

Vellocatus strode over and placed a rough hand on the surface of the crystal.

*It is warm and it does pulse but is it enough? I must trust my Queen.*

"My dear Vellocatus," said the Queen as she moved towards him, "we will die either way. If we fight Venutius we will surely perish. If Lord Alaric assists us we will win or we will die if he abandons us. The odds are stacked against us and I will do everything in my power to improve them."

"Even," said Vellocatus but he was stopped by an acid remark from Cartimandua.

"Yes, even consorting with Beelzebub himself if I must. They were here, working on the detail. Does that not tell you something?"

Vellocatus was beaten, he knew, and fate would hand him whatever it now desired; he would have to deal with it, as he had when it placed Queen Cartimandua into his hands from his master, King Venutius.

*Let the game begin.*

*

Malham Cove is the remains of a waterfall formed when the glaciers that covered most of the Shires during the great ice age melted. It must have been an impressive sight; a long curved

## Chapter 1: Fend for Yourselves

limestone cliff with a virtually limitless volume of water pouring over its edge to create the valley in which Queen Cartimandua and her entourage now camped.

At the top of the curved cliff face were limestone pavements and Malham Tarn, a deep lake and remnant of the glacial retreat. The waterfall was long gone and water from the tarn wended its way through caves eroded deep underground to emerge in two separate and unconnected streams to form the small and insignificant Malham Beck.

A servant was collecting water and horses were drinking from the stream. The water gatherer looked down the valley towards the village of Malham and shuddered. He could not see the village from his vantage point in the cove for it was masked by the forest of the Elven, a taboo place for his kind. The servant carried the water back to the collection of tents that formed the Queen's temporary home for her meeting with the Dämonen. They had arrived on time; the new moon was to be this evening and the meeting with Lord Alaric was the following day at noon.

*

Noon arrived without ceremony and so did Lord Alaric. The first that Queen Cartimandua and Vellocatus knew was that the light faded around them and their entourage was stilled, unable

# Chapter 1: Fend for Yourselves

to respond to any threat, perceived or otherwise.

The Queen heard a voice; Vellocatus did not.

*You wish your mate to be involved in these discussions?*

"You mean Vellocatus, I presume. Yes, I do."

*I am Lord Alaric and ruler of the Shires of York. You have something of mine and you will pass it to me and you will do so now.*

Both the Queen and Vellocatus heard Alaric and they snatched a glance at each other as his voice penetrated. Albert was at Alaric's side as he spoke to the Queen and so was Baron von Brunhild, Alaric's strategic advisor and a thoroughly bad sort, thought Albert.

*This isn't going well. He should listen to me and not von Brunhild. I will take a risk.*

Albert materialised before Queen Cartimandua and Vellocatus and the Queen bowed her head in recognition. Alaric would be furious, he knew. Albert took over the conversation.

*Lord Alaric has the power, if he so wishes, to take what he perceives as rightly his. You understand that these crystals were taken from us by others but they are rightly ours. You have no choice but to release the third crystal to our care. Lord Alaric will take it if you do not.*

# Chapter 1: Fend for Yourselves

The Queen paled and Vellocatus, with a soldier's instinct, went to draw his sword, a useless weapon in the circumstances. He was unable to move his hand and he knew that he was well out of his depth.

"This is treachery, High Priest, we have an understanding."

It was Lord Alaric who spoke, encouraged by von Brunhild.

*The Dämonen does not make treaties with the lesser species.*

*This isn't going well,* thought Albert, *for once I believed that Alaric understood. Obviously not.*

Albert tried to take control again and he sniffed loudly before attempting to commence. In Dämonen and beside him in the great hall, Albert sensed Lord Alaric's wings start to unfold as his vexation grew. Baron von Brunhild positioned himself between the High Priest and Lord Alaric. He was not going to allow Albert the floor. The Baron was powerful but not as powerful as the High Priest. The battle between them commenced, witnessed by the hapless humans, caught up in a power struggle that they had no hope of comprehending.

The Baron materialised in front of Albert's apparition at Malham Cove. His representation was comically grotesque.

*Couldn't he do better than that?*

The Queen stepped backwards and Vellocatus interposed himself between his ruler and the Dämonen, a futile gesture,

# Chapter 1: Fend for Yourselves

well intended.

Albert grasped control.

*Stop.*

With a mighty jolt of power aimed at von Brunhild, the High Priest removed Brunhild's apparition from the scene. Only Albert's was left.

*I will pay for that, I'm sure, but not yet, for I have the plan, not they.*

Albert's image smiled at Queen Cartimandua, now very pale and shaken. She was not reassured by the too perfect representation of Albert before her. She was confused but she too had a plan and it was better than Albert's, or so she thought.

Vellocatus was scared; his army and means of defence rendered inert for the duration.

Albert sensed Alaric move beside him, pushing von Brunhild aside. Albert thought that the Lord was going to intervene.

*Leave me to handle this, Lord.*

As yet, Albert did not wish to confront Alaric's great power and the Lord knew it. Lord Alaric controlled his energy and he ruled with a light touch but it was always clear who was in charge. Alaric trusted his High Priest and Albert was now relying on that ancient bond. Baron von Brunhild, though, was livid.

# Chapter 1: Fend for Yourselves

The Queen picked up the leather pouch and opened it to reveal the Crystal of the Veil. Albert felt the stretching of Lord Alaric's wings beside him in the great hall.

*Now is my chance*, thought Albert.

Albert moved close to the Queen and touched her hand.

*It is now or never.*

Whilst touching the Queen, Albert enacted his magic and the crystal dissolved, reappearing in the great hall.

*I have it.*

What happened next was not foreseen, but immortality is like that. The Queen removed her hand from Albert's chilling touch.

"It is yours," said the Queen, "but the second is mine. You shall not have it for this treachery. Be gone."

Albert's plan was unravelling, for he could do nothing without the Queen's compliance, or that of another mortal. These were the restrictions of the Dämonen exile and the Veils being closed.

*We have the third crystal. How do we retrieve the second? She will not co-operate now.*

*

The scene faded and Albert was, once again, beside Lord Alaric, the Baron on his far side. Looking up, Albert could see

# Chapter 1: Fend for Yourselves

the ire in von Brunhild's eyes and the horns on his head glowed red. Albert returned the resentment in gesture and then turned to look at Alaric.

*He's calm. That's surprising.*

"I may have miscalculated," said the Lord, after a moment's contemplation and the Baron stared at Alaric, disbelieving what he was hearing.

"Yes, Lord," said Albert.

"What do you mean?" blurted von Brunhild.

"Just that," said Albert, "the Lord has been badly advised."

Lord Alaric glanced briefly at his High Priest before saying to the Baron, "If you would be good enough to leave us alone. I will call on you soon."

Von Brunhild glared at Albert, turned sharply and, dispensing with formality, stormed from the room.

"I will deal with him later," said Alaric, "Now, Albert."

"Yes, Lord," said Albert.

"I think I have misjudged you," said Alaric.

"Not just myself," said Albert.

"Meaning?" said the Lord.

"You have overestimated our powers in the Shires," said Albert.

"With the Veils closed you mean?"

## Chapter 1: Fend for Yourselves

"Yes," said Albert, "you know that we can do nothing without the co-operation of humans. They are our conduit. I thought that you knew this."

Lord Alaric looked thoughtful.

*He's thinking but he's not contrite.*

"I doubt if the Queen would give us the second crystal willingly. We seem to have suffered a setback?" said Alaric.

"We?" said Albert, "Yes, Lord, we have indeed."

# 2 – Elven

Tanyl was tall, even for an Elf and his poise and beauty were legend. Like most of the Elven his skin was fair, eyes blue and hair blond; in Tanyl's case he wore it to his shoulders and he tied the front strands behind his head with a coarse leather twine. He was with his companion, Ioelena, an Elf of the same age as Tanyl, young but wise beyond her years. She was slight with long legs and arms and her hair was plaited and circled her scalp being neatly tied with green vine, interlaced with yellow flowers. Their home was in the Elven forest, called desolate by mankind but, for the Elven, nothing could be further from the truth, for it held abodes of intricate detail. They were so sheer that they could not be seen by the human eye, even if it dared to gaze upon the forbidding forest; folklore decreed that they would do this only once and it kept them at bay.

"They have been here, desecrating the cove," said Ioelena.

She was seated in the forest glade, protected by a magic sheen whilst the sun trickled down through the leafy canopy. Tanyl's slight form paced the neat space formed by the clearing as he replied to his consort.

"They have the third, I understand, is that correct?"

# Chapter 2: Elven

"Yes, Tanyl, they have the third. The female ruler has betrayed her kind."

"Who is this?" said Tanyl.

"The human, Queen Cartimandua. They arranged to meet, apparently," replied Ioelena.

"It has been a long time since the Dämonen have soiled the earth and something that they could not do without the help of the Queen. Did she realise the consequence of her actions?" asked Tanyl.

"She was cornered. The protection she received from Rome has been withdrawn with the retreat of the centurions. You know of her rift with Venutius and her mating with Vellocatus?" said Ioelena

"Yes, the desires of mankind, always their failing," said Tanyl, and he continued, "but now their travails are impacting the Shires and the existence of the Thridings themselves."

"They invited them, expecting a treaty," said Ioelena.

"A treaty? From the Dämonen. These humans are bereft of sense. The Dämonen cannot be trusted, as we know to our cost," said Tanyl.

A comfortable silence ensued as both Tanyl and Ioelena mulled over their thoughts. It was Ioelena who broke the peace.

"They have the first and the third and they must not retrieve

# Chapter 2: Elven

the second crystal. They cannot proceed without it but, once they have it, they can open a Veil and then our task will be difficult."

"Do we know the whereabouts of the second?" asked Tanyl.

"No," said Ioelena, "but I am told that the human Queen holds this knowledge. I have not sensed the second in my lifetime, which is, of itself, strange."

"A dilemma," said Tanyl, "for which we will need the assistance of a Council, I fear."

Tanyl was referring to the Elven Councils, the ruling groups of the Elven who sat together to provide guidance on difficult matters; this was one.

*How could we lose the twelve? We had them in our hands and our responsibility was to protect those with sentience. We failed and that may cost us all our freedom.*

"The remaining nine, Tanyl," said Ioelena, "are they safe?"

"They are said to be," said Tanyl, "but so, we thought, were the first three. Time is tight now. These Dämonen have the first and third Crystals of the Veil. They can do nothing without the second but, if they retrieve it, their power will grow in the Shires and Diabolus will be able to enter the other domains. A new dark age will descend upon us."

*I fear that I know what must be done.*

# Chapter 2: Elven

"The Council of Eight it is. Shall I ask for it to be assembled?" said Ioelena.

"That would be wise," said Tanyl.

"I will do it now".

Ioelena left the glade and faded into the surroundings. Tanyl was alone, listening to the sounds of the forest, a sound he loved.

*

The Elven Councils respected the magic numbers of 2, 8, 20, 28, 50, 82, and 126. The Full Council included Elven Elders and numbered 126 representatives. Members were often consulted but rarely met. The Quorum Council, as it was called, was of eight members, rotated annually with participants taken from the 126 Elven Full Council.

The Quorum Council deliberated on an issue first; difficult issues were referred to each upper Council in turn until they were resolved. The number two was also important; Tanyl and Ioelena were the Council of Two and, for the duration, were the implied rulers of the Elven.

The Quorum Council met in the Elven Court, an exquisitely carved building in a forest clearing and protected by a magic sheen.

Ioelena had explained to the Council her reason for calling a quorum session and there was a mumble of conversation circling the table at which they were all seated. Tanyl gave his opinion too, when requested by Ioelena. Elven Councils were civilised affairs and Llarm spoke first when Ioelena had completed her discourse.

"Do we know how the human got hold of the Crystals of the Veil?"

"We do not," said Ioelena, "and we do not know of the location of the remaining nine either."

Llarm was an Elf of some experience; towards the end of his life of several hundred years, he had knowledge of a time when the crystals were in Elven custody. His lined face and tired eyes betrayed his age and his speech was slurred as he spoke.

"I have no personal memory, you understand," Llarm said, deliberating, "but I know of others, sadly no longer with us, who did. You know of the Crystal Venture?"

He looked around.

*Of course they do, every Elf knows of this.*

"The Score Council of the Elven went on a great adventure throughout the Shires, covering most of the wapentakes in all of the Thridings, North, West and East."

The Score Council was the Council of twenty; a convenient number guaranteed to achieve an objective, or so it was thought.

"Their quest was to find the Crystals of the Veil, before the Dämonen did. They travelled far and consulted with all of God's creatures, even mankind. Although their journey was arduous and long," Llarm stopped and looked around before continuing, "and you know that we lost two dear Elven, they achieved their goal and collected all, yes all, of the Crystals of the Veil."

"What happened to the crystals that they found?" said Alanys; she was younger than Ioelena and new to the Council, within the previous year. She had short hair and a full forehead that spoke of her intelligence.

"That, Alanys, is a very good question and the answer to this is that nobody seems to know. The crystals were brought back here and placed under a magic seal but they escaped."

"Escaped?" said Harik, a warrior Elf, his hair tied in a pony tail with a metallic clasp, known for his great prowess but with a short temper.

*Yes, told like this it does seem odd.*

"Yes, escaped. The crystals removed themselves from the captivity of the spell and they have not been seen again by any of the Shire's creatures, until now."

"How long did we have custody of the crystals?" asked

## Chapter 2: Elven

Elidir, a middle aged Elf of some standing; his accomplishments were legend. He was shorter than the others, stocky for an Elf with a lined aristocratic face, long nose and greying hair.

*Custody? The crystals are nobody's property and no one can own them.*

"Custody does not reflect their status, Elidir; even the Dämonen cannot call the crystals theirs. We had them as our guests for half a generation I would estimate. This may seem pedantic but the crystals cannot be contained. We learnt this from our attempt to do just that. Only the crystal chamber and one other place can hold the crystals and that is because they want to be there. If the crystals are in the chamber, the Veils will be activated; then we have real issues."

"Forgive me," said Alanys, "this is quite new to me. Tell me of the Veils and why they are such a threat."

"Start with the Dämonen," said Elorø, a matronly Elf and ancient in years.

"Yes," said Llarm, "they are devils, a dark force in the Shires, under the control of Diabolus, but only nominally. I digress, sorry, a habit of mine. They have great power but their ability to use it is limited, especially where sentient creatures are concerned."

# Chapter 2: Elven

"Like us," said Harik.

"Indeed," said Llarm, "and all mortals in the Shires. They have been seeking the Crystals of the Veil for thousands of years under Lord Alaric's jurisdiction. For our purposes, they are immortal, but not without their weaknesses."

*I must reach my point, stop prevaricating.*

"The advantage they have over all others is that they have the crystal chamber; they can contain the crystals. They require three crystals to create a Veil and there are four veils. The more Veils they have, the more powerful they become."

"They now have crystals one and three, is that correct?" said Alanys.

"Yes, that is right," answered Llarm, "but only the first is secure. Let me explain."

Llarm went on to explain that the crystal chamber requires the crystals to be in the correct order and that the third crystal cannot be placed into it until the second is found.

"So, Llarm, I understand that the crystals are free spirits, if I may use that term, but what I don't understand is what happens to them when they escape from their containment," said Elidir.

"If I may interject, for I have information not known to Llarm," said Tanyl.

Harik exchanged glances with Tanyl; Harik was becoming

impatient.

*We need to reach a conclusion. Llarm will ramble on, if I let him and he knows not of the caves.*

"What I am about to tell you is knowledge that is available to but a few, for having this insight is hazardous. You must never repeat this to another," said Tanyl and he looked around, "The crystals returned to the White Scar Cave, near Ingleton in the West Thridings; they originate from these caves and we, the Elven, created them. Only certain of the Elven know of this; such knowledge is too dangerous. If the crystals remain in their place within the caves for a millennium, they will be absorbed into the fabric of the caves and will be no more. Then the threat of the Veils will be revoked; we will be safe. This is the only other place that the crystals choose to be."

"Is that the case?" said Llarm, "Does that mean that the nine remaining crystals are in the cave, assuming that the Queen of the Brigantes is telling the truth and she has possession of the second."

Alanys shook her head and said, "Forgive me, this is a lot to take in. How did the crystal come into the Queen's possession, and, if she found the second, does she know of the cave?"

"We don't know the answer to that, Alanys," said Ioelena, "but our assumption has to be that she has no knowledge of the cave."

"That seems a dangerous assumption," said Elidir, "for the Queen of the Brigantes may have all of the crystals; she may have retrieved them from the cave already."

"That is unlikely," said Tanyl, "you know of White Scar Cave?"

Only Llarm nodded.

"Let me tell you about it," said Tanyl, "for it is enchanted and guarded by the Dragon Tanwen and her brood. I don't believe that any human would survive an exploration of the White Scar Cave. Tanwen is the Fire Manon, the word the dragons use for Queen, for only females have fire in their breath."

*I am starting to drift too; bring this to a conclusion.*

"Let me sum this up. The name 'cave' does not do White Scar justice for it is a long expanse of thousands of paces. It has many natural features of hanging stalactites and rising stalagmites, underground waterfalls and a great cavern. It is almost impossible to enter unseen by the dragons. The crystals will be there, I am sure and I do not believe that the Queen of the Brigantes has the second crystal, though I may be wrong."

"She had the third, Tanyl. What makes you think that she does not have the second?" said Harik.

# Chapter 2: Elven

"I do not sense it like I sensed the third."

"And nor I," said Ioelena.

"I am not sure that I know where this is leading," said Elorø, "the crystals seem to be at home in White Scar Cave or in the crystal chamber. If they remain within the cave they are lost to the Dämonen and, over a considerable period of time, will be absorbed by the cave. Why do we not just leave them there?"

Alanys interrupted, "How did they return to the cave? Llarm said that nobody knew this, but you seem to have additional knowledge."

Tanyl replied, "The Dragon Tanwen. She retrieved the twelve crystals from our custody and returned them to the cave. This is not widely known. The dragon's duty is to keep the crystals safe until they can reach the crystal chamber. Although the Dragon Tanwen is not aligned to any side in this, and certainly not to the Dämonen, they will not intervene unless the crystals wish it."

"Wishes it?" said Harik, "Does a crystal have a soul?"

"Some of us can sense the Crystals of the Veil, as can the dragons, and they are much more sensitive to their aura than are we."

"What do you want of us, Tanyl?" said Elorø, for she was becoming tired of the endless deliberation.

## Chapter 2: Elven

Ioelena looked at Tanyl and they exchanged information by a fleeting glance. It was she who spoke.

"We must find the second and return it to the care of the Dragon Tanwen and her brood."

# 3 – Duplicitous Queen

Queen Cartimandua and her army had returned to the City of York and the troops were camping outside of the city walls. Her Roman protectors were making haste in their retreat from their colony of Britanniae. The Queen had word of an army, led by Venutius, heading from Parisi lands towards the Brigantes. She understood him to be in the East Thriding, in the Wolds so she knew that his progress would be rapid. He had joined forces with the Angles, who had a reputation as fierce fighters. The Romans had fought alongside them, rather than face their combat. The Angles had been rulers of Roman Britain, except in name, and they were not likely to relinquish that role. A power vacuum was being created by the withdrawal of Rome; the Angles intended to fill it.

The Queen knew that she would lose if she faced Venutius with her army. Vellocatus, ever a soldier, wanted to fight.

*He knows no better. It is his idea of honour. I will not lose and I will do whatever it takes to defeat Venutius.*

"This is what I want you to do and this evening," said Queen Cartimandua to Vellocatus.

They had been discussing tactics in the Queen's Lodgings; she was not staying with the army.

## Chapter 3: Duplicitous Queen

"Here are a list of their names and their abodes. They are to be rounded up and kept under guard. They are not to be harmed. I want them alive."

"Who are these people, my Queen?"

"They are all relatives of the King," she said, "or close confidantes."

The Queen gave Vellocatus a knowing glance.

"We will raise the stakes," the Queen continued, "for we have five days, maybe six if we are lucky, before we have to face his army."

"Meanwhile, I want a messenger to be sent. One of your bravest."

"Yes, it will be done. Where is he going?" said Vellocatus.

"To the caves and he must ride like the wind."

"You mean the dragon's cave?"

"Yes, my love, to the dragon's cave."

*He will die*, thought Vellocatus.

"For what purpose?" said Vellocatus.

"You will have to trust me."

"As always, my liege, with my life."

"Before I do this duty, my Queen, tell me one thing," said Vellocatus.

"If I can," answered the Queen.

## Chapter 3: Duplicitous Queen

"These crystals, are they part of this?"

"They are, and the second will play a most crucial part in our success over Venutius."

"Can you confide in me?" said Vellocatus.

"You look hurt, my dear," said the Queen, "but you have no need. I will tell you but there are some things that should not be broadcast afar. What I will tell you is as such."

*He has been so faithful and a consort who has exceeded my expectations, in many ways. I owe it to him.*

"Before I do, let me tell you that I will need a second messenger and it will be a dangerous mission, to Venutius and his army. What he will take with him is of grave importance that only you, my dear, will I entrust. I will expect you to return, so take no unnecessary risks."

"Your first messenger will need to start soon for he needs to travel nearly twenty leagues, over difficult and boggy terrain. Please see to it first and then I will confide in you the most important of information. See that he carries a messenger bird too. I need to know that he arrived."

"I will do this now and I will send two soldiers, to ensure its success. I will also see to your other order, the King's relatives, at the same time."

"So be it," said the Queen as Vellocatus departed for the

## Chapter 3: Duplicitous Queen

camp.

Queen Cartimandua dismissed her servants soon after her consort left her lodgings. She removed her fine gown, dressed herself in the clothes of a peasant and walked into the city, towards the river to the only bridge. She was scrutinised by an Angle guard as she crossed; the Romans were thin on the ground. Just before the fortress, she knocked on the door of a rich merchant's house, styled as a Roman villa. It was answered by the occupant's servant who looked askance at the peasant woman standing before him.

"What do you want," he said to the Queen.

"Give your master this, if you please," Queen Cartimandua replied.

She handed the servant a message; it bore the seal of the Queen of Brigantes and the servant recognised it immediately.

"My master," the Queen said, "says it is of the utmost importance."

"My master is about town," said the servant, "but will return shortly."

"You must give it to him as soon as he returns, please."

The servant was starting to become suspicious. He heard the sound of Queen Cartimandua's noble born speech; her disguise was thinning.

# Chapter 3: Duplicitous Queen

*Who is she? She is not who she appears. Recognition.*

"Is will be done, you have my word, my Queen," said the servant.

"Thank you. You must tell nobody but your master that I have been here."

The Queen turned and left as the servant closed the door.

*

Godric returned to his home. His merchant business was becoming more difficult with the withdrawal of most of the Roman legions. Lawlessness was on the rise and he was paying more in bribes to keep his consignments safe. He yearned for a return of the certainties offered by Roman rule. It had gone for good, he knew, and a new order was being created.

*I need to be on the winning side. I am too old for changes like this.*

Godric looked around his hall, searching for his servant. He sorely needed something to eat and drink. He was just in his fifties, a fine age for the time, and he'd had a good life, up until now.

*Why were they leaving? Why so quickly? It is most inconvenient.*

His servant arrived and took his master's outer tunic from him.

## Chapter 3: Duplicitous Queen

"We have had a visitor, master," said the servant.

Godric looked up. Mostly, his servant was invisible to him, necessary to his life but of no consequence to him.

"Who?" Godric said.

"It was the Queen."

"The Queen, here?"

*What is she thinking, to come here so openly?*

"She was disguised," said the servant, "but I recognised her. She said not to tell."

"Good advice. What did she want?"

"She gave me this for you."

The servant handed Godric the sealed letter from Queen Cartimandua.

"Thank you," said Godric and he retrieved a silver penny from his pocket and handed it to the servant.

"I saw nothing master. I will bring you some sustenance," said the servant and he left Godric alone.

Godric took the letter and walked into his dining room; he used it also for his business dealings: counting takings, accounting, meeting with his clients or other merchants and for his rare bouts of entertainment. His house styled in the Roman fashion where people sprawled to eat, a practice he held in disdain. He had no wife and no children; they had died

# Chapter 3: Duplicitous Queen

during childbirth when he was young and he had not wanted to remarry.

*It has taken me time but I am now comfortable in my own company. There are so few one can trust.*

After seating himself at the table head, Godric tore open the seal of the letter to reveal the Queen's delicate hand.

*"My Dear Godric,*

*"I hope this finds you well for we live in strange times. I must tell you of grave news: Venutius has amassed an army and is travelling with it from the east to fight against us. I am taking steps to ensure his defeat and, Dear Godric, I hope that you can trust that my judgement on this is sound."*

*My faith in you is unquestionable; I would die for you.*

*"I entrusted into your care something of great value, locked in a lined box and I am sure that you have it safe. I am sending my commander, Vellocatus, to collect it. I would ascribe its care to nobody else. He will collect it today and I know that I can rely upon you to ensure that he, and only he, collects it. He will have a letter bearing my seal and will carry the ring, the one you so generously gave me as a gift, as you and he have not met before.*

*"I know that I can depend upon you and you have my fondest affection."*

## Chapter 3: Duplicitous Queen

The Queen signed the letter in a swirling script.

\*

Vellocatus stood in the hall of Godric's home, a sealed box under his arm. He looked back as he cleaned his sword. Godric and his servant were prostrate on the floor. Vellocatus patted his pocket; the key to the box was there, as was Godric's gold.

*The Queen's instructions were clear. I was to retrieve the box, dispose of Godric and not open the casket until I am at Venutius' camp. Ensure that I return and do not fail.*

Vellocatus opened the door and stepped outside where people were milling around, busying themselves with their daily chores. He mounted his horse and, with a soldier's purpose, crossed the bridge and turned east.

# 4 – Female Power

It is little known by humans that the male dragon is much smaller than the female and that only the female has the ability to scorch the earth and her victims.

Padrig was the smaller male whilst his mate Tanwen, the Fire Manon, was the larger female. Padrig was flying high, heading home to the White Scar Cave. It was close to midday and the air was clear. His senses were acute and much better than any other creature of Earth. Below him he spotted two horsemen galloping recklessly across the moorland circling Ingleborough, the highest peak that Padrig could see. Their trajectory was clear: White Scar Cave, there could be no doubt.

*Why would a human want to risk this journey? It has to be important, to them.*

The revelation cause Padrig to beat his wings just a little faster and he gained ground on the horsemen. He swooped lower for a better view.

*There are two of them and not well armed. They must be lost, fools or worse.*

Padrig made good progress and was at the entrance of the cave well before the horsemen were in sight. He called out to Tanwen; he had news.

# Chapter 4: Female Power

Eoforwine and Wilfrid were the messengers ordered to the dragons' cave. They had been riding since early morning and the sun was now at its zenith; it was becoming hot. They had stopped their horses for a break near a stream; both they and the men needed some water and food.

Eoforwine was a taciturn man, not prone to idle chat. He was battle scarred and the lines across his face enhanced his rugged appearance. Wilfrid was slighter in build than Eoforwine but was a tough man who had seen many skirmishes. Vellocatus had chosen well.

Eoforwine pointed towards the north west, up into the sky and said, "The dragon, he flies. He is smaller than I feared."

Wilfrid looked skywards to view the retreat of Padrig towards his home in the cave.

"He will have seen us," said Wilfrid, "they see well, for leagues."

"We must be on our guard," said Eoforwine.

*Though I do not know how we can fight a dragon and win.*

"We still have the runes," said Wilfrid, "they have not slipped from the saddle?"

He smiled at Eoforwine who said, "I am pleased, for we would have to abscond otherwise."

57

## Chapter 4: Female Power

They both had reservations about their mission but they kept their counsel.

"Come, we must go. We need to be close by nightfall," said Eoforwine.

They mounted their steeds and ploughed on towards an uncertain fate.

*

Dragons were, by nature, solitary creatures and Padrig's return was to a lukewarm reception. Tanwen tolerated her mate of countless years but the unbridled affection of their earlier years was well behind them.

"Did you say that you had news?" said Tanwen, folding her wings into place as they moved through the narrow passages towards the cavern where they lived with their adolescent daughters most of the time.

"It can wait until we are back," said Padrig, adding, "how are Buddug and Dona?"

"They have been fine," said Tanwen, "they are becoming a handful, that's for sure."

Their daughters had reached an age where they needed their own independence and Tanwen was keen to encourage them to find their own caves. Padrig was not so sure.

*I would be left with Tanwen. What a prospect!*

## Chapter 4: Female Power

They entered the large opening of the chamber and Buddug and Dona were waiting for their father. They blew large flames into the air in delight at his return.

"Now stop that," said Tanwen.

The girls flapped their wings at their father who did the same in return. They loved their diminutive parent.

Buddug was the younger by a couple of years and slightly larger than Dona. Both were now formidable dragons and as fierce as their mother when they set their mind to it. Padrig knew that they would have to leave soon but he was going to do no pushing.

*They can leave when they wish as far as I am concerned.*

"What have you caught today? I'm hungry," said Padrig.

"You are always hungry," said Tanwen.

"Leave papa alone, you are always picking on him," said Buddug, her nostrils flaring and emitting dark smoke, on the edge of fire.

*She's such a miserable Fire Manon.*

Tanwen was having none of it and flicked the unruly child with her tail and sent her rolling across the cave floor.

"Now, mama and you kids, pops is home and I would like a bit of civility if you don't mind. I also have some news that might be of interest to you. Something that might sate those

## Chapter 4: Female Power

pent up frustrations."

They tucked into a wild boar, lightly roasted, dragon style and, as they ate, Padrig spoke.

"As I was flying over Ribblesdale, I spotted some riders and they are heading our way. I flew a little lower so that I could see them better and they look like Brigantes to me. You know, that Queen who tried to negotiate some kind of agreement with you mama a few years back. What was her name, now?"

"Cartimandua," said Tanwen, "Queen Cartimandua. She had some courage that one, if misplaced."

"Well, there was never a chance of a treaty, of course. Now where was I? Ah, yes, these horsemen. Whilst I was away, I learned of a plot by this Queen to join forces with the Dämonen."

He was interrupted by Tanwen who shrieked and blew a long stream of fire into the air.

"The Dämonen, those devil henchmen of Diabolus, what was she thinking?" said Tanwen.

The girls looked at each other, puzzled. Their father explained whilst mother looked on impatiently.

"It seems," Padrig continued, "that a Crystal of the Veil, or maybe two, have been found by this Queen."

"Ah," said Tanwen, "two of the missing three."

## Chapter 4: Female Power

Buddug and Dona knew all about the crystals; it had been their birthright to care for them and they knew of the crystal's folklore.

"The first is not missing and now, it appears, nor is the second," said Padrig, "I know that the first and third are with Alaric, Lord of the Dämonen."

The female dragons flamed together at this news and Padrig flinched.

*I wish I could do that.*

"He needs only the second, and he has a Veil," said Tanwen, her nostrils still smoking.

"We must stop them," said Dona.

"Indeed we must and having the third without the second is a weakness for them," said Tanwen, adding, "is there more papa? You mentioned the second crystal."

"The Queen is saying that she has the second too," said Padrig, expecting further fire but none came.

*No more theatricals please.*

His three females said nothing, so Padrig continued, "I had heard that she is sending messengers to us and the horsemen may be them."

"You are well informed, as always, Padrig," said Tanwen.

"It is what I do," Padrig said and he felt warm inside for

## Chapter 4: Female Power

praise came rarely from his mate, "so, girls, if you could, perhaps, desist from incinerating these humans, at least until we have their message?"

*

The horsemen, Eoforwine and Wilfrid, reached White Scar Cave at nightfall and made their rough camp. They were not going to risk confronting the dragons until the morning. They lit a fire, ate their meagre rations, fed the messenger bird, for it would be flying back in the morrow, and turned in early. The night was cool but dry and both slept fitfully.

*Who knows what fate awaits us?*

The rune stone had been placed between them for it gave warmth and light and kept away others that may have wished harm to them. This would be the last night of its protection. The camp fire burned slowly and they took turns to tend it during the night.

Unknown to them, from the top of the scar, a dragon watched them sleep and observed the rune stone as it glowed its soft light. He could not decipher its meaning from his position on the cliff but he knew that tomorrow he would. He must be patient, he had the time that these humans did not.

*

"Padrig, you know that you cannot", said Tanwen, "and you

## Chapter 4: Female Power

know why too."

Padrig was irritated. He wanted to meet with the humans and listen to the rune's message.

*It's always the same. I provide the information and they take the glory.*

"They have a rune stone, did you say papa," said Dona, her nostrils smouldering.

Padrig looked up at her.

*My, how she's grown and how fierce she is now.*

"Yes, my sweet," said Padrig, "and it is full to brimming."

"When was the last time we heard a rune play?" said Buddug, "We must have been very small."

Tanwen mused and a fine trail of white smoke from her mouth betrayed her deliberations.

"The message must be of some importance," she said, "it is not easy to create a rune. Not easy at all and they must have had help."

She looked at her children and her nose wrinkled. Padrig knew that look.

"No fireworks, you understand? I want to hear the message and the humans are the key for the runes this time. No humans, no message. I would like them whole and I want them to return home, terrified but alive to tell their kind of what they saw."

## Chapter 4: Female Power

"Yes mama," said Buddug.

*I hope they understand. They are such reckless children.*

*

Eoforwine took the folded slip of parchment and tied it to the bird's leg. He stoked its head gently and then placed the bird between his hands. With a brief thrust, the bird was gone. It circled once and then turned south east towards York and their Queen.

*It is time.*

"Eoforwine, there is no need for us both to die here," said Wilfrid, "I will do this. You return."

"No friend. Soldiers do not desert their mates and you know that. We are in this together. Besides, you are lousy with a sword."

Wilfrid grinned at Eoforwine and they clasped hands together as a sign of camaraderie.

"Swords against dragons," said Eoforwine, "we can't lose."

Wilfrid retrieved the rune stone and they walked towards the entrance to the cave.

*What do we do now? Knock?*

The runes will do the calling, their commander had said. They placed the rune stone between them on the floor and it flipped into the vertical.

## Chapter 4: Female Power

*It looks like our tombstone.*

They both heard the noise. Sweat was trickling down each of their foreheads. Wilfrid placed his hand on his sword, ready for action.

*A useless gesture but I feel better for it.*

The rune stone started humming. It was a beautiful, rhythmic tone.

*Elf music. The music of ecstasy but the last sound you hear, they say.*

Eoforwine felt a dribble of perspiration run down his side. He was trembling but trying not to show his fear.

*My senses, they are so intense.*

A column of smoke preceded the three dragons: Tanwen, the Fire Manon and her daughters Buddug and Dona. Padrig watched from above them at the top of the cliff, unnoticed by the men.

*Pure theatre. She's good, I'll give her that. This should scare them rigid!*

Tanwen exited the cave first and was flanked by her offspring. She released a tiny flame from her mouth; a small show of her power. Buddug and Dona behaved and kept their furnace cold.

*So far so good.*

## Chapter 4: Female Power

Wilfrid's heart was beating quickly, as was Eoforwine's. The rune stone took control. Tanwen looked down at the pint-sized humans below her.

*How puny they look.*

Runes danced from the stone and arranged themselves in front of the dragons. Padrig watched as characters formed their communiqué for the creatures of fire. Then, the runes sang an anthem that was beautiful and mesmerising; most of all, it was calming and tensions diminished as the runes sang their Elven melody.

The runes delivered their message and each of the dragons heard it, including Padrig high above. Its importance was unquestionable. The tune faded and the stone's power died with it. No longer adorned with runes, nor glowing, the stone now looked no different to the thousands of others littering the ground.

Tanwen turned to the humans and she gave a single order to them.

"Go."

They did not need to be told twice.

# 5 – The Chancer

Vellocatus rode alone due east towards the Wolds of the East Thriding of the Shires. The going was tough as the land was wet and boggy and Vellocatus had to retrace his steps on more than one occasion. He knew that Venutius would be meeting similar terrain and took some comfort from this; Vellocatus was confident that it would delay Venutius.

The Wolds were no place to dally. Vellocatus had heard of the Malevolence but had never experienced it. It was said to roam the featureless expanses of moorland and seek out travellers.

*Folklore, only folklore.*

Vellocatus knew that it would take over a day to reach Venutius' camp so he would have to spend a night out on the Wolds; they were damp and uninviting places and a light mist hung over them as Vellocatus continued his ride.

*In this terrain I will have no advantage of height. I may come upon Venutius haphazardly and then I will die and will fail in my duty and my Queen. I must be careful.*

Vellocatus had brought with him a Crier, a bird of the Elven, as his scout. It circled overhead and Vellocatus held out his arm. The bird descended, spread its wings to slow itself and

67

## Chapter 5: The Chancer

placed its feet deftly on Vellocatus' outstretched limb.

"Your pace, further half day," said the Crier, "alter course south east. Care. Big army, move slowly."

Vellocatus fed the bird from his rations and thanked his scout.

"Don't like place. Evil about," said the bird and it stretched its wings and soared into the air.

*Will I see you again, friend, tomorrow?*

Nightfall slowed Vellocatus and he was forced to make camp. He checked the casket strapped to his horse; it was still intact, the key safely in his pocket. He freed the horse from its chattels and searched for wood for a fire but there was none. This would be a long, cold night. The horse ate from vegetation around Vellocatus and he supplemented it with some hay; it was not enough, he knew.

*I expect so much from her. She gives it, always.*

Wrapped in a light blanket, Vellocatus slept restlessly, his sword not far from his side. These were unruly lands and a solo traveller was easy prey.

*I need to sleep. The morrow will be a challenge.*

The early hours came and Vellocatus sensed it first, before the horse whinnied. He was alert immediately, casting aside the blanket as he stood, sword in hand.

## Chapter 5: The Chancer

"Who is there, show yourself."

*Nothing.*

The chill was intense.

*It's early morning, of course it is cold. No, this is different. It is just superstition.*

Vellocatus turned. Still nothing except the frigid air.

Faint at first, the outline of a woman appeared, her features indistinct but her posture betrayed her age. The horse snorted but did not bolt.

"YOU HAVE NO NEED OF THAT," said the apparition, "IT WILL DO YOU NO GOOD."

Vellocatus stood his ground, "Who are you? Are you the Malevolence?"

"SUCH AN UGLY NAME," said the Malevolence, "NOT ONE I WOULD GIVE MYSELF."

Involuntarily, the sword dropped from Vellocatus' hand and, in a distracted manner, he watched it fall.

"Am I to die at your hands?"

"IT WOULD BE A SHAME FOR A SOLDIER SUCH AS YOU TO DIE IN THIS WAY. DO YOU NOT THINK?"

What does that mean? Am I to die or am I not?

"YOUR MISSION. IT INTERESTS ME."

*Was that a yawn? Surely not.*

## Chapter 5: The Chancer

"Forgive me, I haven't slept for a thousand years and I get so tired sometimes. Tell me of your journey. I don't get to speak to many people."

"It seems to me that you know much already."

"You are very perceptive, young man, but tell me anyway. Leave nothing out, for I will know."

The Malevolence indicated that Vellocatus should be seated.

*This is bizarre.*

Vellocatus started talking and in a way that he hadn't done before; he bared his soul and he wasn't sure why he was doing it. His hopes, his dreams, his successes and his failures; they all flooded out. His mission. He tried to cover up its purpose but he could hide nothing from this spirit. His soul was exposed to her. Finally, spent, he stopped and watched the spectre in front of him as she watched him.

"You see, that wasn't so bad, was it?" said the Malevolence, "don't you feel cleaner inside now?"

"Now, I am to die?"

"Your obsession with death, it belittles you. I'll spare your life because I see the love you hold for your Queen. She does not deserve it, the conniving little weasel, but for you it is real."

"Do not talk of my Queen in this way."

## Chapter 5: The Chancer

"Ah, the blindness of deep love. My outburst is of nothing and you are brave, if foolish."

*I am helpless. She could end it here if she wished. I must do her bidding.*

"What is it you want of me?"

"You have given me more than you could know already," said The Malevolence, "for it is many years since I have heard such words and felt such things. I am indebted to you, Vellocatus, Queen's Envoy. I will help you in your mission, for I see beyond what you see; Queen Cartimandua's real purpose and it serves the greater good, though she does not know this."

*I don't understand. I am but a soldier and must do whatever it takes to obey my orders and fulfil my duty.*

The chill subsided and The Malevolence faded again into the background. Vellocatus' horse looked towards him. It was dawn and time to continue his journey.

Vellocatus was tired after his restless night but the adrenaline flowing through his veins pushed him on. His steed was also charged for it rode like it was possessed. He'd been warned by the Crier bird that the army was near but Vellocatus heard them before he saw them.

*The unmistakable sound of an army marching.*

## Chapter 5: The Chancer

He had to find cover for he could not risk being seen by Venutius or his supporters. Nightfall was the time to complete his mission so he tarried in the shadows, conscious of a presence at his shoulder but unseen when he looked.

Venutius' army was vast, covering a column of a half a league from its head to tail. Venutius led on foot and his armour bearer, the role of Vellocatus before the rift in their relationship, held his horse. Few of the foot soldiers had steeds and the going was tough in the difficult terrain of the Wolds. Vellocatus admitted to himself that the sight before him was impressive and he feared for his Queen's safety should they succeed in their mission.

*I'm not sure what I am to achieve here but if my Queen thinks it will help then I must see to it.*

He followed the convoy discretely for the remainder of the day until, just after dusk, they made their makeshift camp for the night. Vellocatus watched as the army machine operated; soldiers were fed, fires lit, weapons cleaned and sharpened and a multitude of activities done to keep the army a fighting force.

Vellocatus fed his horse and himself from his skimpy supply; he wished he'd had time to hunt, or even lay a fire. He was cold as the darkness draped over him. The dots of light from the army fires were his only reference points against the

## Chapter 5: The Chancer

blackening sky.

Then it was time. He took the key from his pocket, threaded it onto a thin strap of leather and placed it around his neck. Then, he removed the box from his filly and placed it under his arm to carry to the encampment.

*It has arrived again; the horse brays and the chill intensifies. Malevolence is emerging from the gloom.*

"You are back."

*A stupid thing to say.*

"IS THAT NOT OBVIOUS?" said Malevolence but not in a malevolent manner.

"I LIKE YOU."

Vellocatus was puzzled but he could not reciprocate.

"I SAID THAT I WOULD HELP YOU AND SO I SHALL."

"How?"

"YOUR MISSION IS TO CONCEAL THE CONTENTS OF THE CASKET SOMEWHERE IN THE ARMY COLUMN, IS IT NOT?"

Vellocatus nodded.

"I WILL BE YOUR CONCEALMENT. I WILL TAKE THE SECOND CRYSTAL OF THE VEIL, FOR THAT IS WHAT THE BOX CONTAINS, AND TRAVEL WITH THE CONVOY TOWARDS YORK. I DO NOT EXPECT THEM TO ARRIVE."

"You are kind," said Vellocatus, "but this is my duty and I

# Chapter 5: The Chancer

have been ordered not to fail."

"You are also to return, safely. Open the casket & give to to me."

Vellocatus was reluctant.

"I could take it easily, but I would prefer if you were to comply with my request."

*I cannot do this. It would be dereliction.*

"What were your orders? Think before you reply."

Vellocatus contemplated a response and then said, "To intercept Venutius' army, open the box, remove its contents and conceal it within Venutius' column."

"Give me the casket and you will have accomplished your mission. You may travel to the camp with me if this makes you more comfortable."

*I will do this.*

"It shall be," said Vellocatus, "and I will travel with you."

Vellocatus took the key and opened the casket. It was lined with a material he had not seen before and embedded was an exquisitely carved stone, the Second Crystal of the Veil. It was so different to the third that he'd seen before. It glowed and sparkled; each face was indented as if a template for the other Crystals. It was truly resplendent and its power evident.

"It is even more beautiful than I had imagined."

## Chapter 5: The Chancer

The Malevolence waved her arm and the Crystal floated through the air and was one with her; now it was invisible, at least to humans.

"WHAT BETTER A WAY TO CONCEAL IT? I WILL NOT FAIL YOU VELLOCATUS, QUEEN'S CONSORT."

She allowed Vellocatus to follow her to the edge of the camp and then told him to watch but remain where he was.

"RETURN TO YOUR QUEEN ONCE THIS IS DONE."

Vellocatus watched as Malevolence walked into the encampment and straight towards a sentry. For a moment Vellocatus looked on in terror as Malevolence slid into the guards body; the defender was now absent and Malevolence occupied the space where his soul had been. When she left him again, he would be dead.

*I must trust her now for there is no choice. It is time for me to go.*

# 6 – The Elven Voyage

"Did you sense it?" said Tanyl, flicking back his flowing hair.

"It was sudden and potent; then its power waned but I could still feel it. The first time in how long?" said Ioelena, stretching her long neck and peering into the forest.

"At least a millennium and it is time," said Tanyl, "but we must honour the Elven ways. Two or eight?"

"Not the Quorum Council," said Ioelena, "for Llarm and Elorø could not make a journey. We need to respect their years."

"Harik is headstrong but a good warrior and the rest of the Quorum would be beneficial," said Tanyl, "we need to choose two from the Score. Llarm and Elorø will understand, I am sure."

"It is to the East Thriding we must go, to the Wolds and we must make haste. The Crystal of the Veil is moving towards York. We will not be able to intercept it easily there," said Ioelena.

"The plan is set. Let us enact it," said Tanyl and he flapped his translucent wings ready for the flight.

\*

## Chapter 6: The Elven Voyage

They flew in formation high above the Wolds: Tanyl, Ioelena, Alanys, Elidir and Harik were joined by Quinn and Avae from the Score Council.

Quinn was a young Elf with a powerful presence and combat experience. With his considerate manner, he complemented the headstrong Harik and was a welcome addition to the team. Avae was a healer, or sister as they were known, in her middle years and everyone hoped that her skills would not be needed; better that she was present than otherwise. Unusually for an Elf, her hair was copper red, unruly with natural curls.

Harik's experienced eye saw Venutius' army first. The Elven were flying high and invisible to the Commander. Tanyl sensed the Crystal of the Veil strongly as did Ioelena and excitement rose, tinged with apprehension.

*It is close, but where?*

Harik indicated that they were to descend, behind the army column so as not to be seen. The landing was uneventful and the Elven team regrouped.

"Something is not quite right here," said Avae, "I sense danger and evil."

"I sense it too," said Ioelena, "and it is mixed with the Crystal, though I don't know how."

"Look," said Elidir and he pointed towards the horizon, "we

77

# Chapter 6: The Elven Voyage

have company."

*

"Are you sure that I can't come along?" said Padrig and he sighed.

*Keep your ear to the ground, that's all I ever get; never anything exciting.*

Tanwen blew a small flame from her nostrils and tiny wisps of smoke followed after the flame had been extinguished.

"You know that you can't, Padrig, now don't be awkward. Humans need big fiery dragons and you just don't fit and don't sulk."

"Oh, can't he come mama?" said Dona," he looks so miserable."

Tanwen threw her daughter a look that would have frozen hell; her meaning was clear.

"Now, keep the cave safe whilst we are gone," said Tanwen, "and don't go far. Come on you two, we've a job to do."

She flapped her wings and Padrig felt the air rush past his face as his mate ascended into the sky, followed by Buddug and Dona. Soon they were small dots in the heavens heading east.

*Stay safe.*

The journey was arduous and the air turbulent as they flew

# Chapter 6: The Elven Voyage

over the open moors. On they went until they hit better laminar flows over the Wolds of the East Thriding of the Shires of York. Far below them, they saw the half a league long column of Venutius' force moving slowly westwards. Tanwen ordered her daughters to ride the thermal up-thrust and circle so that they could converse, something that was easy for a dragon.

"That is our target," Tanwen said, "spare nobody but secure the crystal. Can you sense it?"

"I can," said Dona, "but it is odd."

"Odd?" said Buddug.

"I know what Dona means," said Tanwen, "it feels masked."

"Yes, and can you feel it, the evil presence?" said Dona.

"Now that is tangible," said Buddug, not wanting to be left out of the conversation.

"We have company too," said Dona, "over there."

Dona pointed with her nose towards the south and the three dragons watched eight small Elven figures drop from the sky and land behind the army line.

"The Elven," said Tanwen, "that can only mean trouble. Come."

She broke the circle and plunged towards the army column; she could be seen clearly by Venutius and his men but that was of little concern to her or her daughters. They dropped from the

## Chapter 6: The Elven Voyage

sky and landed to the south of the Elven. They looked tiny in comparison to the dragons but Tanwen knew that their powers were considerable.

*

Venutius saw the dragons as they landed and was hoping for the best, that they were not seeking him, but feared the worst. He called for his second in command.

"I want bowmen and the best swordsmen to hand. If we have to fight them, I want to win."

Justus, the son of a Roman merchant and of mixed birth looked at his commander.

*We cannot fight dragons; we will all die.*

"Yes, Sir," he said.

"And send a scout. I want to know what they are doing and where they are heading," said Venutius.

*This is all I need.*

The army marched onwards, their progress more urgent now. The scout returned and the news was bad; there were dragons and Elven and they were conversing.

"Justus, I have not heard of this before; dragons and the Elven do not like each other. Why would they meet?"

"I know not, Sir" Justus said.

*Of course you don't. But, nor do I.*

# Chapter 6: The Elven Voyage

*

Tanwen felt distaste talking to the Elven; despite the historic concord, they were not her kind.

"Why are you here?" she said.

Ioelena took the lead.

*Female to female may help the discourse.*

It didn't assist as dragons were unable to see gender differences in the Elven.

"Probably the same as you," Ioelena answered obliquely.

"Don't trifle with me," growled Tanwen and a trail of smoke drifted from her nostrils.

The Elven seven moved closer to Ioelena. Magic was in the air and the dragons detected it.

"There is no requirement for aggression, Tanwen, Fire Manon and mother of the dragons. Our dispute is with the humans and not with you and your kind. Remember too, that we have an alliance."

The magic thickened and Tanwen and her children could appreciate its energy.

*There will be spent blood if we continue. We must find an accommodation.*

"Very well," said Tanwen, "my daughters, Buddug and Dona, and myself have no quarrel with you. Our accord is not

# Chapter 6: The Elven Voyage

in question but has not yet been put to the test."

"Can we understand why you are here, if you please," said Ioelena.

The mood lightened and the magic softened again, ready but no longer a suffocating presence. The two species faced each other, both formidable but the stalemate had been averted.

"We are here to retrieve the Second Crystal of the Veil," said Tanwen.

"You know of it?" said Ioelena.

"We do. We had a messenger from the human, Queen Cartimandua, that it would be here. We know that to be true."

"As are we and we also know that the Crystal is here," said Ioelena.

The Elven group shuffled uncomfortably. Tanyl felt that Ioelena was leaving them exposed and he went to talk but Ioelena quietened him with a spell.

"The Crystal must be returned to White Scar Cave for it belongs there."

"The Crystal will decide where it belongs, I believe," said Ioelena.

"Your knowledge is excellent," said Tanwen, "and I assume that you refer to the Crystal Chamber."

Ioelena nodded.

# Chapter 6: The Elven Voyage

"The Crystals choose not to reside in the chamber whilst it is in the possession of the Dämonen."

"But, Tanwen, Fire Manon, the first Crystal is already resident in the Crystal Chamber and the Dämonen now have the third," said Ioelena.

"So I understand," said Tanwen, "but this is what we must do."

"We?" said Tanyl and Ioelena glanced at him.

*I know that look. I must remain mute.*

"Yes, we," said Tanwen, "we each have our roles to play in this."

"SO DO I," said a voice.

They hadn't noticed the chill.

"Who are you?" said Tanwen.

"This is The Malevolence," said Ioelena, intercepting the newcomer's reply.

"NOT THE NAME I WOULD CHOOSE, BUT NO MATTER," said Malevolence.

She held out her hand and the Second Crystal of the Veil drifted into it. Dona expelled a flame into the air and Tanwen gave her a frigid glance.

"I'm sorry about my daughter," she said, "she is rather impulsive, just like her father."

## Chapter 6: The Elven Voyage

Tanwen made play to grab the crystal.

*It's mine by right.*

"Not so fast," said Malevolence, "I have a request for you before I let you have the Crystal. I also wish to learn of your plan, Tanwen. You said that both the dragons and Elven have roles to play. Please elucidate."

Tanwen looked at the group of little Elven before her and at the apparition holding her prize.

*What can I lose? We cannot achieve this alone for we cannot enter the land of the Dämonen and the Elven have shown that they cannot hold the Crystals captive.*

"It is like this," said Tanwen, "only we can secure the Crystals away from the Dämonen and you know that they have limited powers in the land of sentience whilst there are no open Veils. What you may not know is that, until a Veil is opened, we cannot enter the land of the Dämonen, but Elven can."

Ioelena looked at Tanyl. She did not know this and none of the eight had acquired enough Elven knowledge to be sure that the Fire Manon was telling the truth.

"I can see that you doubt what I am saying but I tell you that I do not lie."

"She tells the truth," said Malevolence, "the Elven

# Chapter 6: The Elven Voyage

CAN ENTER DÄMONEN."

"I am prepared to believe this revelation," said Ioelena, "but tell me what you wish us to do."

"We will retrieve the Second Crystal of the Veil but you, the Elven, must return the First and Third Crystals to us," said Tanwen.

"From the Dämonen?" said Ioelena.

"Yes, but that is not all."

"Go on, please," said Ioelena.

"You must destroy the Crystal Chamber so that it can never be used. For, if it is ever populated with the twelve Crystals, we will enter a new dark age that will mean slavery for all sentient creatures."

"Such an undertaking, it is impossible, is it not?" said Ioelena.

"DIFFICULT, YES. IMPOSSIBLE, NO," said Malevolence, "BUT BEFORE WE CONTINUE. I NEED SOMETHING FROM YOU, TANWEN, AND YOUR DAUGHTERS. THEN YOU MAY HAVE THE CRYSTAL."

"Yes, what is it?"

"YOU MUST DESTROY THIS ARMY, COMPLETELY."

"Is that all?"

*

## Chapter 6: The Elven Voyage

Padrig scanned the sky for the return of Tanwen, Buddug and Dona. The image was indistinct at first, even with Padrig's dragon sight. Then it was clear; he could see his mate and children returning and he was overjoyed. He watched them land.

*Skilful as always. I have taught them well.*

"Papa," said Buddug, followed closely by Dona, "we've had the time of our lives."

"I hope you've prepared a meal, Padrig, I'm famished," said Tanwen and, with some pride, she displayed the Second Crystal of the Veil.

"One down, two to go," she said.

Inside the cave, they ate a hearty feast and Padrig listened to their tales.

"What I don't understand is the Elven bit, and this Malevolence woman. Just explain that again," said Padrig.

"Oh, Papa, it's easy," said Dona, "mama persuaded the Elven to change their quest. They are now going to Dämonen to fetch the other two crystals and destroy the chamber."

"That's the bit I don't understand. Why would the Elven agree to that and to go to Dämonen too? Nobody would do that willingly," said Padrig.

"I used the end-of-civilisation argument," said Tanwen.

# Chapter 6: The Elven Voyage

"Oh, that old one," said Padrig.

"What would you suggest as you are so smart?"

"The old ones are the best ones, my dear," said Padrig dismissively, knowing that he could not win an argument with Tanwen.

"Look, Padrig, the Elven have agreed to the odyssey and Malevolence has agreed to help them."

"She has?"

"Yes, I am not sure why but we will achieve what we want; the Crystals will be safe and in our care and we will be rid of the Crystal Chamber for good."

"Does anyone know what will happen when the chamber is destroyed?" asked Dona.

Tanwen and Padrig stared at each other. They didn't know.

# 7 – A Plan Adrift

"You have word?" said Queen Cartimandua.

She looked apprehensive, uncertain even; this was a rare emotion for the Queen but it was fleeting and her composure was restored.

"The scout has returned, my liege," said Vellocatus, "and the news is good."

"Pray, tell me," said the Queen and her face betrayed her relief.

"Venutius' army has been destroyed, as you had planned, by the intervention of the Dragon Tanwen, the Fire Manon. It is no more and it can no longer threaten you."

"Thank the Lord," said Queen Cartimandua.

"There is more," said Vellocatus.

"Go on," said the Queen.

"The scout said that he saw the dragons in discussion with the Elven."

"He saw the Elven and he survived? Elven and dragons do not like each other."

"Nor us," said Vellocatus.

"Indeed. The scout was brave to have stayed. He should be given a commendation for this."

# Chapter 7: A Plan Adrift

"It will be done," said Vellocatus, "but prey my indulgence for I have yet more."

The Queen glanced at Vellocatus and raised her eyes.

"I need to tell you of what happened to me at Venutius' camp for you to understand."

"This is intriguing," said the Queen.

"If you please?"

Queen Cartimandua nodded and Vellocatus proceeded to tell the Queen of his experience with The Malevolence and that he had been forced to place the Crystal of the Veil in the care of the apparition. She listened in silence.

"Are you telling me that you disobeyed my orders?" she said when it was clear that Vellocatus had finished.

He explained that he had not and that he had watched as Malevolence had taken the soul of a guard and embedded herself and the Crystal within Venutius' army camp.

"I felt that I had obeyed your orders at that point and you ordered me also to return."

Queen Cartimandua paced the room, deep in thought.

"So be it," she said finally.

The meaning of this statement was unclear to Vellocatus but he took it to be supportive and continued.

"The scout saw also the apparition of Malevolence

consorting with the dragons and Elven. He said that they looked like they were hatching a plan of some sort."

"Interesting. I guess that we do not know what the plan was," said the Queen.

"No, they spoke in the ancient tongue," said Vellocatus.

"What of the Second Crystal of the Veil?" asked the Queen.

"It is with the dragons," said Vellocatus.

"A pity, but the price we had to pay."

"You have served me well," said the Queen, "as always, King Vellocatus."

Vellocatus blushed.

"All will know that you hold this title: Vellocatus, King of the Brigantes, ruler of the Shires."

*

Albert stood on the ledge outside the Great Hall of Dämonen. He sniffed.

*This is going to be a difficult day.*

He folded his wings, knocked and entered, tail between his legs, as was expected.

*Pointless practices.*

In the hall were Lord Alaric and Baron von Brunhild and an Alder was pecking at a dead rodent on a perch near the window.

# Chapter 7: A Plan Adrift

*Von Brunhild, just what I need.*

The rituals of greeting were dispensed with quickly and Lord Alaric spoke.

"The Baron tells me that we have lost the Second."

"Very careless of us," said von Brunhild.

*I'm sure he is sneering.*

"Dragons, they have it now, again," said the Alder and she continued eating her prey.

Lord Alaric looked towards his bird and reached out a claw to stroke its head. The Alder snapped at the Lord and he placed a strong talon into the bird's open jaw.

*A show of strength that Alaric wins every time; the games he plays?*

The Lord grew tired of tormenting the Alder and returned to the conversation.

"Von Brunhild tells me that Elven were involved in an exchange. Is this true High Priest?"

"What else did the good Baron tell you?" said Albert, becoming irritated.

"Forgive me," said the Baron, "it is not my duty to act as messenger for the Lord?"

*An obtuse slight.*

Albert sniffed, deliberately.

## Chapter 7: A Plan Adrift

"It is not," said Albert, "but what do you know Lord, for I do not wish to waste your time."

Lord Alaric looked to the heavens.

*Sometimes they act like children.*

"Tell me what you know Albert," said Alaric.

Albert acknowledged the olive branch being offered; unusually, Lord Alaric had used Albert's name, rather than his title, and in Baron von Brunhild's presence.

"Queen Cartimandua is playing to win," said Albert, "but is playing a dangerous game. She has used the Crystal as a pawn in her little endeavour for power. It seems that she sent a scout party to White Scar Caves with some runes."

"Runes," said Alaric, "the dragons would not be able to resist them. Clever."

"They informed the dragons of the whereabouts of the Crystal and they went to retrieve it. Cartimandua wanted rid of the army that was threatening her and the dragons did her bidding, albeit unwittingly."

"I care not for the fortunes of humans," said the Lord, "but what of the Crystal?"

"The Baron is correct," said Albert and he sniffed, "the Second Crystal of the Veil is now with the dragons and out of our reach. Without human intervention, with the veils closed,

## Chapter 7: A Plan Adrift

we are stymied."

Lord Alaric's wings twitched slightly, betraying his vexation.

"Forgive me," said von Brunhild.

"Yes," said Albert.

"Does that not create a dilemma for us? What do we do with the Third Crystal?"

"Von Brunhild is correct, High Priest," said Alaric, "Crystals are difficult to contain and they have a mind of their own. The Third rejects the Crystal Chamber without the Second and I can feel its pull away from us already. But, tell me of the Elven."

"Elven, Dragons, the Evil one," squawked the Alder.

Albert looked over at the bird as it tugged at the foot of what looked like a rat.

"Something surprising has happened," said Albert.

Baron von Brunhild raised his eyebrows.

"Go on," said Lord Alaric.

"The Elven sensed the Crystal's presence. They were aiming to rescue it from the humans. They had no knowledge of the dragon's quest. Both seemed to arrive together."

"Interesting," said Alaric.

"Yes," said Albert, "but even more interesting was that they entered into conversation."

"Unprecedented," said the Baron.

# Chapter 7: A Plan Adrift

Albert sniffed at the interruption and said, turning his head towards von Brunhild, "They have an alliance, Baron," and then continued, "We can't be sure of what was said but, not long after they had started, they were joined by The Malevolence and she had the Second Crystal."

"The evil one," said Lord Alaric.

The irony of a demon calling another malefic was not lost on Albert.

*He means the powerful one. He still fears her return.*

"What is clear is that the Elven abandoned their enterprise, leaving it for the dragons to complete. Curiously, Malevolence handed the Crystal over to the Fire Manon once she was sure that the human army had been stopped. The Elven left before the deed was accomplished."

"Malevolence?" said Alaric.

"She faded back into the Wolds."

"I do not trust her and will not use her real name here," said Lord Alaric.

"We should not," said Baron von Brunhild, "she was banished to roam the East Thridings eternally."

"She has been seeking a way to return to Dämonen since that time," said Albert, "something we should not permit."

"We can handle her," said Lord Alaric dismissively, "but the

Elven are a different matter. We should not miscalculate again."

*

Ramm had been an Angle warrior for the Romans, now departed; they'd called him a mercenary but he saw himself as a proxy ruler. He'd witnessed the power vacuum form and he was the man to fill it. His army was of first rate fighters; nothing less would do for self proclaimed King Ramm of the Angles. Most of his adult life, he had fought alongside Virgil, his second in command and they were brothers in arms, if not biologically. Since the departure of Rome he'd amassed tens of thousands of followers, all loyal to their King. He'd seen to their needs and their pillaging, starting at the East, had ensured them wealth, company, new recruits and supplies.

Now, he gazed upon his major prize. The city of York, with all of its riches, lay before him, defended by the ragtag army of Queen Cartimandua of the Brigantes and her mock King Vellocatus.

*She and her army will be easy prey and I will make her my Queen? Vellocatus must perish for there can be no other outcome.*

# 8 – The Door

Tanyl and Ioelena had decided to consult their elders.

"We do not speak of these things," said Elorø, her lined face betraying her age and concern deepening the contours.

Llarm nodded, blinked and looked pensive.

"I am sorry, Elorø but we need to know. Tanwen, the Fire Manon was most explicit."

"What exactly did she say?" said Llarm, his sad eyes dulled, reluctant to expose ancient truths.

It was clear from their discomfort that both Elorø and Llarm had knowledge but that they wished to keep their counsel. Tanyl sighed.

*We're getting nowhere.*

"That the Elven could enter Dämonen and that we should return all of the Crystals of the Veil to the dragons," said Tanyl.

Llarm drew in his breath with a hiss.

"And that we should destroy the Crystal Chamber," added Ioelena.

At this, Elorø stood and flayed her arms around as she spoke, "Have we lost our senses?"

The clearing filled with Elorø's magic and a second shield spread around them, adding to the cloak already present.

96

# Chapter 8: The Door

"What is this?" said Tanyl.

"Such discourse hold peril," said Llarm, "Elorø is protecting us."

"Protecting us, from whom?" said Ioelena.

"There are things of which even the Council of Two have little comprehension," said Elorø, "and I will tell you but only under this duplex veil. You must give me your word that no other of the Elven will learn of what I will say. I need your assurance as members of the Council of Two."

"You have it," said Ioelena.

"Both of you," said Elorø.

"Of course, you have my commitment," said Tanyl.

"Thank you," said Llarm, releasing a pent up breath.

"The Dämonen will know of your meeting with the dragon for they have spies everywhere. That is their priesthood's job and the High Priest takes his role very seriously. The Barons of Dämonen are Lord Alaric's secret police; a check-and-balance on the priesthood. There is a tension between the two Directorates, as they are called, and Alaric encourages it. Power trickles down and there is no consultation like our Elven Councils. Lord Alaric wears his crown lightly most of the time but, when it is needed, he is ruthless," said Elorø.

"You know that the Dämonen are effectively contained

within Dämonen?" said Llarm.

"Yes," said Ioelena, "their ability to influence the world of mortals is very limited."

"All of that is true," said Elorø, "to a point. They have learned a few tricks over the last few thousand years. You remember, they did manage to get hold of two crystals."

Tanyl and Ioelena nodded and looked thoughtful.

"That means that they have interacted with our world," said Tanyl.

"Yes, but can you see that they needed humans to help them. Humans are so easy to manipulate, after all," said Llarm.

"Council of Two," said Elorø, with aplomb, "this exile that the Dämonen suffer is our doing; we expelled them and we created Dämonen."

It was now Tanyl's turn to draw his breath through his teeth.

"How?" he said.

"It is of little value for you to know how the Elven did this," said Llarm, "only to be aware that it happened. In any case it is forbidden knowledge."

"Why is this so? If we are to complete this challenge we will need all of the learning of the Elven, won't we?" said Ioelena.

"The quest is yours," said Elorø, "not the Elven."

"Are you saying we should forget about it?" said Tanyl.

# Chapter 8: The Door

"I think we are," said Llarm, "some things are better left undone. This may be one of them."

Elorø became ponderous while Ioelena and Tanyl were left with their own thoughts. It was some time before Elorø spoke again.

"You cannot un-remember what you know," she said, "so I cannot agree with Llarm. You must honour the commitments you have made and we must help you understand better the risks you are taking."

Elorø smiled at Llarm.

"Wise as always, Elorø," he said.

"First, though, let me tell you of the other in your chance meeting, Malevolence. She is an exile of Dämonen and has a desire to return. She was Lord of Dämonen prior to Lord Alaric and the price of the Dämonen's exclusion was her exile. She is trapped in the Thridings of the Shires of York. She will do only what is in her own interest; anything she may have done for you or others will contain self-interest. She is personified evil, however she may seem to you."

"The spectre you saw was a representation; she showed you what she wanted you to see. She shifts shape at will," said Llarm, "but you will know she is there because she trails coldness wherever she goes."

## Chapter 8: The Door

"Do not trust her," said Elorø, "or it will be your downfall."

"Tell them of what the dragon implied," said Llarm to Elorø.

"I was coming to that," she replied, "give me a chance. We have a Door leading to Dämonen and it has been sealed since their exile. It leads to a cavern that cannot be accessed from outside, only through the Door; from there, an opening leads to the Labyrinth of Dämonen. To gain access to Dämonen means traversing the Labyrinth and there are snares; a wrong turn will lead to death and your magic will be useless in the maze. You will need the ancient map of the Labyrinth and your wits; not everything is shown on the plan and some aspects you will have to work out for yourself."

"If you make it through," said Llarm, "you will then face the Dämonen but you should have an advantage by then, if you survive."

"What is that?" said Tanyl.

"You will have the protection of the Shield of the Labyrinth. It is not foolproof but it should defend you against all but Dämonen's most powerful sorcerers."

"Like Lord Alaric and his High Priest," said Llarm, "for you will be on your own against their potency."

"If you fail, the consequences could be grave," said Elorø, "for a Door is two way, what can go in, can come out and that means the Dämonen, if they can fathom the Labyrinth. Right now, the Door is closed and the exit from the maze into Dämonen is sealed from the inside. If you open the seal there is the possibility of the Dämonen using the Door themselves."

"But, as Elorø said, they would have to cross the Labyrinth."

"Where is this Door?" said Tanyl.

Elorø and Llarm glanced at each other.

"It is in the New Elven Forest in the Harthill Wapentake of the West Thridings of the Shires of York."

# 9 – The Angles

Queen Cartimandua looked down from her horse at the turmoil that was York, her City and her stronghold. It was now in the hands of the self proclaimed King of the Angles, Ramm. She despised him.

*He is a renegade and has no noble birth.*

What King Ramm did have was a strong army of fighters and the Queen's entourage had been soundly defeated in battle. She had been lucky to escape with her life. Such fortune had escaped her Consul, Vellocatus, and he had fallen in order to allow her to escape.

*I owe it to him to survive and regroup to fight again for our honour. The land of the Brigantes will be mine again, I swear it.*

The Queen urged her horse on; she and her few remaining soldiers rode on to the Wapentake of Harthill. She had allies there and was confident that they would assist her.

The journey was gruelling; the weather worsened the further south they travelled. On they rode until they arrived at the East Bar of the small city of Danum on the River Don, one surrounded by a ditch and protected by an earthen rampart and wooden palisade. At the gate she asked the guard to show her to an important merchant of the city. The soldier looked at her askew until she showed him her Royal Seal.

"Ma'am," he said, "follow me."

*

The Merchant Leng had ensured that the Queen was comfortable and supplied with her needs. Her soldiers has been billeted and horses stabled. Leng was seated at a long table in a vaulted room and accompanied by his old friend and business accomplice, Rice.

"What is she doing here Rice?" Leng said, "I don't want this kind of trouble, especially now."

"What does she want?" asked Rice.

"I don't know yet," said Leng, "but it will involve money. With the nobles, it always does."

"I have heard that York has fallen," said Rice.

"When? I have not heard," said Leng.

"My guard, he told me. The Angles are in charge, something we'll have to get used to, I think," said Rice.

"You know Rice, you may be right for they have moved into the East and now control much of the Shires," said Leng.

Rice poured some ale into an earthenware mug and refilled Leng's flagon. Leng was deep in thought.

"You give me an idea," said Leng.

# Chapter 9: The Angles

"Before you go on," said Rice, "I have something else to tell you. I found this out only yesterday."

"Intriguing, please tell."

"You remember Godric? We did some work with him. You recall, he smoothed a path for us in York."

"Unmarried, dour chap?" said Leng.

"That's him. Well, he and his servant were found and shall we say that they were in no fit state to talk," said Rice.

Leng knew his friend's euphemism; it was one he always used when someone had died.

"How?" said Leng.

"Foul play," said Rice, "and the Queen's Council was seen entering Godric's premises."

"You think," said Leng.

"Certainly, I think," said Rice, "and I also think that you, and probably we, should be very careful around Queen Cartimandua. She is a big risk to us, on many levels."

Leng was ponderous again but Rice interrupted him.

"What was the idea you were going to mention?"

"It follows on pretty well from what you've said, Rice," answered Leng, "I was going to say that we must be aware of the new order of things and not burn our bridges."

"Meaning?" said Rice.

# Chapter 9: The Angles

"We must be sure that we support whoever is going to win," said Leng.

"Is that not going to be our titled Queen?" asked Rice.

"Unlikely, and not at all if we intervene," said Leng, "after all, even the Angles will need our services and I really don't care which of these power hungry tyrants I'm serving. They all look the same to me but my money is going on the strongest and that means Ramm, not Cartimandua. The sooner the winner is proclaimed the quicker we can get back to the business of filling our coffers. Rice, all I am suggesting is that we tip the balance in Ramm's favour and do it quickly."

*

"Pass my thanks on to your master. You may go now," said Virgil.

When the messenger left, Virgil stood and made his way to Ramm's quarters. He knocked loudly on the door.

"Yes, who is it?" said a voice from the other side.

"It's Virgil."

Ramm opened the door. He was holding a sword, which he sheathed as Virgil entered.

"Can't be too careful," said Ramm.

"How is it now Virgil, are we secured?"

"We have York in our hands and our troops now hold much

# Chapter 9: The Angles

of the Shires. We're seeing some resistance, but it is dwindling. By tomorrow the Shires will be ours," said Virgil.

Ramm smiled.

*Then the difficult part starts. Administration of the Shires. I will leave that to Virgil. He'll organise that.*

"That is good," said Ramm, "see to the rest in the morrow. We need to collect some taxes and consolidate our rule."

Virgil nodded; they made a good team.

"I have had a message from the West Thriding," said Virgil.

"From whom?"

"An influential and wealthy merchant. He sent a messenger."

"We will need his like if we are to prosper," said Ramm.

"Yes," said Virgil, "I thought so too."

"The message?" said Ramm.

"He has Cartimandua," said Virgil.

"Has he, by the Lord," said Ramm, "then we must relieve him of this burden."

"Do not let your heart rule your head," said Virgil, "she has a following and is a risk to us. She is better if she is no longer a problem."

"She is better if she is allied to us and what better a way than through marriage?"

"She will not marry you, Ramm. You should not try to force

her for I think it would be a grave mistake," said Virgil.

*There is nobody else that could talk to me in this way but he means well for me. I would trust him with my life – indeed thus has it been many times.*

"I know you mean well my friend. Pray, let me think about this. Tomorrow, we will discuss this again."

*

Padrig was at the Crystal Wall in a cavern within the White Scar Cave that was the dragon's home. He came here for some time alone; the entrance was small so Tanwen and his daughters were too big to enter. He looked at the Crystal Wall and its twelve spaces for the Crystals of the Veil. Two were empty, of course, but the remainder held crystals safely in their holders. The indents in the wall to house the intricately shaped crystals were arranged in groups of three, each representing a potential veil for the Dämonen.

The first row of three housed only crystal two; position one and three were empty. This row was of concern to Padrig as the only crystal present was glowing brightly; the other rows were dormant.

*It is distressed; something is wrong with this crystal.*

*

Queen Cartimandua was seated at a dressing table and

adjusting a brooch on her blouse. Leng had found her a lady-in-waiting who was seeing to her needs; Leng had made himself scarce and this irritated the Queen who wanted his help and his wealth to raise an army. She wished to call in some favours too and would demand his assistance. His absence arose her suspicions that all was not well.

*I must be careful.*

The Queen had not seen her soldiers since arriving and made a mental note to find them; she felt vulnerable. She held her weapons close, ready for action if it was needed. She dismissed her servant and walked to the window of her room. A light rain kept most people off the muddy streets. She drew her arms around her for there was a sudden chill in the room. The Queen pulled herself away from the window and turned. In the centre of the room was an elderly woman.

*She's not quite real, more an image.*

Alarm shot across Queen Cartimandua's face but her composure returned.

"Who are you," she said, "and what can I do for you?"

"THEY CALL ME THE MALEVOLENCE," said Malevolence.

"Do they indeed. You have not answered my question."

"YOU ARE MOST CONTROLLED QUEEN CARTIMANDUA," said Malevolence, "MOST PEOPLE ARE FRIGHTENED BY MY

## Chapter 9: The Angles

PRESENCE."

"I am not most people," answered the Queen.

"IT SEEMS YOU ARE NOT. BUT WE ARE WASTING TIME WE DO NOT HAVE. YOU MUST LEAVE."

"Why is that?"

"BECAUSE YOU HAVE BEEN BETRAYED DEAR QUEEN BY THOSE THAT YOU HAVE TRUSTED AND TROOPS ARE CLOSE TO THE SOUTH BAR OF THE CITY. THEY HAVE COME TO TAKE YOU TO MARRY KING RAMM OF THE ANGLES."

"Marry, never! He is no king. He is not of royal blood."

"NEVERTHELESS, IF YOU LOITER FURTHER, YOU WILL MARRY HIM OR PERISH BY HIS HANDS. IT IS YOUR CHOICE."

The Queen thought for no longer than a moment. She retrieved her weapons.

"The south gate, you said. I will make for the East Bar. Can we talk further?"

"IF YOU DO NOT LEAVE THE THRIDINGS, YES WE CAN."

Queen Cartimandua fled the city, leaving everything she now owned behind. She was alone, or so she thought.

"NOW, SHE'S A COURAGEOUS LADY," said Malevolence to an empty room.

# 10 – The Second Crystal

"What is she trying to achieve High Priest?" said Lord Alaric.

Albert was near the window in the great hall next to the Alder's perch, which was now empty. Bits of bone littered the floor; the remains of the Alder's last meal.

"Are you listening?" said Alaric.

Albert turned and his wings rustled a fraction, betraying his annoyance. Alaric raised his eyebrows. He was not accustomed to insubordination. Alaric demonstrated his power and the air crackled with blue arcs of energy.

*I will show him who is the Lord of Dämonen.*

Albert's magical potency was equal to that of Alaric but he wore it lightly and Alaric was still deluded.

*Now is not the time for this.*

"I am sorry, My Lord," said Albert, "I was thinking."

"Did you hear my question?"

"Yes Lord Alaric, I did. Lady Tanja seems to be consorting with the Elven, dragons and humans. There seems to be no consistent pattern to her actions. She helped Queen Cartimandua's mate, Vellocatus, defeat his rival Venutius. Both of these humans are now dead; Venutius at the hands of the

# Chapter 10: The Second Crystal

dragons and Vellocatus during one of the skirmishes that are the hallmark of mankind."

"The Queen, is she dead also?" said Alaric.

"No. That is most surprising," said Albert, "Lady Tanja helped Queen Cartimandua escape. The new human ruler of the Shires, King Ramm of the Angles, had desires for her. A troupe of his soldiers had been sent to apprehend her."

"Most unusual," said Alaric, "for the affairs of man are of little concern to us; they are so fleeting. What can she achieve from her interventions?"

"Your original question, Lord," said Albert, "that was causing me to ponder. I fear that I do not know the answer but I have some suspicions. For Lady Tanja works to her own ends, as you know well."

"Indeed I do," said Alaric, "but the cost was borne by her and not myself."

"It was, Lord Alaric."

Albert answer was diplomatic for Albert remembered well the chaos after the battle for dominance won by Lord Alaric. Even after the passage of time, scars still remained within Dämonen for Lady Tanja was popular and ruled for many aeons.

*I'm sure that Alaric fears her return. So do I, but for very*

# Chapter 10: The Second Crystal

*different reasons; Dämonen cannot survive another leadership struggle.*

"Tell me your suspicions, Albert," said Alaric.

*An olive branch. He is worried.*

"I have no evidence, Lord," said Albert.

"I understand," said Alaric, "but tell me anyway."

"The Elven were discussing something interesting but I caught only a little. An elder of their Council cloaked their gathering; she was concerned lest they be overheard."

"Rightly, it seems," said Alaric.

Albert smiled and fluttered his wings.

"Yes, Lord. What was heard was alarming enough. The Elven wish to return our crystals to the care of the dragons, enter Dämonen and destroy the crystal chamber. What else they spoke of is uncertain."

The air was riven with Alaric's energy again and Albert stepped aside to allow it to dissipate through the window.

"Can they do this?" said Alaric.

"That, I do not know. My suspicion, however, is that Lady Tanja knows how this can be done and she will help them."

"And herself," said Alaric, "for I am sure she wishes to return."

"Yes, Lord. That is my fear too," said Albert, "but let me

# Chapter 10: The Second Crystal

consider this further. There are a few things that are biting the back of my mind."

*

Queen Cartimandua rode on to the New Elven Forest in the Harthill Wapentake. She knew of the mythology associated with the forest; her reckoning was that this would keep her foes away. The weather had improved during her ride but the ground was soft and she had to ride with care.

*No mishaps, for that could prove fatal.*

At the edge of the dense forest the Queen dismounted and allowed her horse to eat; the air was scented, sun warm and a gentle breeze ruffled her hair. Later, she led her steed into the forest through the tall trunks arranged haphazardly, each tree aiming to outdo its neighbour in a contest for the light in the canopy above. Those that failed lived their lives as spindly saplings, awaiting their turn to reach for the sky when one of the giants fell.

*Winners and losers, just like us? Am I the loser this time?*

It was darker in the forest and the noises different to those outside; distant noises and those from the elements were damped but new sounds took their place like the creaking of the boughs as branches rubbed against each other.

*What tales these trees could tell.*

## Chapter 10: The Second Crystal

Although called the New Elven Forest, this was an ancient one and some of the trees were a thousand years old. Stout and tall they stood and they'd endured many frenzied storms. The Queen knew that the forest was managed by the Elven but she'd never seen one of their kind. She knew the folklore: a human who glimpsed an Elf would not live to see another day.

*Just mythology and yet part of me believes it.*

Clearings were few at the edge of the forest so Queen Cartimandua was forced to probe deeper than she'd intended. Her senses were keen; she heard every sound and tried to interpret each. When she came upon the glade it was a surprise to her for she hadn't seen it coming.

*It is good to see the light again and feel the sun's warmth.*

Her plan was in tatters. She'd travelled to seek allies after her defeat at York. Instead she'd met treachery and she could not see how her failures could be reversed. Now, though, she had urgent needs; she was thirsty and hungry.

*

"I tell you Tanwen there is something wrong," said Padrig.

"So you keep saying," said Tanwen, "but what specifically."

"If I knew that I wouldn't be asking," said Padrig.

Tanwen blew a wisp of white smoke from her nostrils and sighed.

# Chapter 10: The Second Crystal

"You know that I cannot fit in there," said Tanwen, "this is your realm. You must sort it."

"You don't need to, for I have it here," said Padrig.

He unfurled his wings and plucked the Second Crystal of the Veil from beneath. Its surface pulsed with flashes of a blueish light. Buddug and Dona looked up; they'd been ignoring their parents, assuming that they were having another of their frequent confrontations. This was different and it had their attention.

Tanwen moved closer to the crystal and placed a claw onto its surface. Their daughters shuffled forward for a closer look.

"What do you feel, Tanwen," said Padrig.

"Ssh," said Tanwen, "give me time, will you."

Padrig looked at his children who gave him a weak and knowing smile.

The crystal ceased its throbbing as Tanwen tried to scrutinise it. She closed her eyes in concentration and flickering flames emerged from her mouth. Time seemed to drag as Tanwen continued her exploration.

Finally, Tanwen removed her claw and the crystal continued its palpitations of light.

"Well?" said Padrig.

Silence.

## Chapter 10: The Second Crystal

"Tell us mother," said Buddug.

Silence.

"It's complex," said Tanwen.

"Yes?" said Padrig.

"Yes, Padrig, Yes," said Tanwen and the gust of grey smoke from her snout showed her annoyance.

Padrig stepped back, expecting the flames to follow but they didn't arrive.

"Well," said Tanwen, "basically, it is lonely. The crystal is desolate without the other crystals. It doesn't want to be here. It wants to be with the others."

"Is that all?" said Padrig, "I knew that already. A child could have read that. I thought you said it was complex."

He walked back further.

*I may have overstepped the mark.*

Tanwen sighed and said, "I am simplifying for you."

"Mother!" said Buddug.

Tanwen delivered a curt glare to her daughter who held her ground.

"Look, we have two choices Padrig," said Tanwen, "we either take the second crystal to the Dämonen or we let the Elven complete their mission and return the missing crystals to us."

# Chapter 10: The Second Crystal

"You are not suggesting," said Padrig but he was not allowed to finish.

"No," said Tanwen, "we can't allow the Dämonen to take possession of the crystals."

"So we have one choice," said Padrig.

"Don't split hairs," said Tanwen.

"We do have two options," said Dona.

Tanwen looked at her daughter and Padrig followed her lead.

"We can go to Dämonen ourselves and bring the crystals back."

"And how do you suggest we do that?" said Tanwen.

"You are the one with the answers," said Dona.

# 11 – Dämonen

"HELLO," said Malevolence.

Alarmed at first, Queen Cartimandua grasped her sword and turned to face the intruder.

"Oh, it's you," she said and re-sheathed her weapon.

"WELL, HELLO TO YOU TOO," said Malevolence, trying not to show her peeve.

*She's a Queen, used to subservience, I guess? Most people fear me and this is quite refreshing.*

"I meant no insult to you. I would like to thank you for your warning, though."

"YOU ARE VERY WELCOME QUEEN CARTIMANDUA, QUEEN OF THE BRIGANTES."

"No longer, it seems."

"I WOULD NOT BE SO SURE, QUEEN. YOUR LUCK MAY JUST HAVE CHANGED."

The Queen looked at the apparition before her; a frail old woman but not quite real. A projection?

"How so?"

"WE ARE FORGETTING OUR MANNERS QUEEN, FOR I HAVE NOT INTRODUCED MYSELF."

"I know who you are," said the Queen, "they call you The

# Chapter 11: Dämonen

Malevolence but I know differently for my nanny told me the history of your world, of Dämonen, and it was fascinating. To think that your kind is amongst us and most have no comprehension of this."

"TELL ME MORE."

"You are Lady Tanja, the wisest ruler of Dämonen, exiled here by Lord Alaric after you lost the war for supremacy. You are searching for a way back."

"YOU FLATTER ME CHILD, BUT FEW OF YOUR KIND KNOW OF THIS."

"My nanny was not of my kind and nor was she of yours; she knew much and she taught me well."

"A SENTINEL, THEN, IN THE LITERAL SENSE."

"Indeed."

"THERE ARE FEW OF HER KIND LEFT IN THE WORLD."

"I believe that you had something to do with this."

"NOT DIRECTLY BUT LET US NOT DWELL ON HISTORY."

"History influences the current and trust or otherwise between us. The Dämonen do not care for mankind. We are mere smudges on their antiquity. Our lives a blink of an eye to a Dämonen; irrelevant, inconsequential, until now."

"MEANING?"

"Come now, Lady Tanja. Would we be talking if there was

# Chapter 11: Dämonen

not a value to our interaction? A value to you?"

"YOU ARE IMPERTINENT, QUEEN."

*But refreshingly honest.*

Queen Cartimandua looked up at Lady Tanja.

*I know how you really look and it is not like you appear.*

"Then tell me. What is it you want of me to have troubled yourself by saving my life?"

"YOU ARE CORRECT ON MANY LAYERS QUEEN AND YOUR SENTINEL HAS TAUGHT YOU WELL. IT IS NO SURPRISE THAT YOU HAVE SURVIVED THE CONTINUING SQUABBLES OF MANKIND, A BLIGHTED SPECIES. I WILL NOT PREVARICATE AND YOUR ASSESSMENT IS ACCURATE. I DO NEED YOUR ASSISTANCE AND YOU WILL BE REWARDED HANDSOMELY."

"How so?"

"I CANNOT RETURN TO DÄMONEN ALONE. I NEED TO BE ACCOMPANIED."

"Myself?"

"QUITE, BUT NOT IN THE NORMAL SENSE OF THE WORD."

"Go on."

"I HAVE THE POWER TO TAKE CONTROL OF HUMANS, ENTER YOU, IF YOU WILL."

Queen Cartimandua betrayed her angst with a sharp intake of breath.

# Chapter 11: Dämonen

"NORMALLY THIS ACT REQUIRES THE SACRIFICE OF THE VICTIM'S SOUL. BUT, I CAN DO THIS LIGHTLY TOO AND THE TARGET WILL USUALLY BE UNHARMED."

"Normally? Usually? You use vague words Lady Tanja and I am assuming that your target will be me."

There was an uncomfortable silence for nearly a minute broken by Lady Tanja.

"I CAN FORCE THIS IF I WISH BUT I CHOOSE NOT TO."

"Your true colours at last Lady Tanja. But, I suspect not, for you would already have done this and with a lesser person. I have some special trait, do I not?"

*Beaten by a human. She'd good. I almost like her.*

"But, I think I have it. I think I know what it is you need. Your kind are exiled, are they not? You have difficulty interacting with our world but you have found a way and you need us, the species you consider to be trivial, valueless, to achieve your goals. That is correct, isn't it?"

"LET US NOT BE ADVERSARIES QUEEN CARTIMANDUA. LET US JUST ACCEPT THAT WE BOTH HAVE SOMETHING THAT THE OTHER WANTS AND LEAVE IT AT THAT?"

"And what do you have that I want?"

"THE RETURN OF YOUR KINGDOM."

*

# Chapter 11: Dämonen

The Council of two Elven left early in the morning. They soared high into a cloudy sky and were soon out of sight of Elorø and Llarm who were watching them depart. Safely under Elorø's silencing spells she spoke to Llarm.

"This is unprecedented and, since the trials, we have avoided contact with the Dämonen."

"There are risks Elorø but what would happen if we leave it all to chance and the Dämonen achieve their ends?" said Llarm.

"I worry," said Elorø, "for Tanyl and Ioelena, of course, but also of the consequences if they fail. Dämonen back in the world is almost unthinkable."

"We must wait and see. Destiny is being set and we are no longer its leading players. May we succeed against our foes."

"May we succeed against our foes," said Elorø repeating the Elven incantation, "and may providence be on our side.

Flying north east, high above Elorø and Llarm, were Tanyl and Ioelena. They flew in silence towards the Elven forest in the Wapentake of Harthill; they'd vowed silence until they were safely through the door and free from the spying eyes of the Dämonen High Priests. The Council of Two was prepared, or so they thought; rehearsed and briefed by the Elven elders until they were reciting their plan flawlessly. Only then did

## Chapter 11: Dämonen

Elorø pronounce them ready.

*

Padrig had returned the perturbed crystal to the Crystal Wall in the cavern, his favourite place, second only to the top of the scar where he could see his beloved Shires. He came to the cavern to take care of his crystals and to think when he was troubled, as he was now. Tanwen had not enlightened him and he now wished that he hadn't involved her. Dona's interjection was playing on his mind.

*Why can't I fetch the crystals from Dämonen?*

His girls had told him about the Elven door and he knew of the forest they'd mentioned.

*But where is the door?*

Seated at a rock, polished by centuries of his pondering, he faced the crystal wall.

*The second crystal, what is it saying to me?*

Padrig remained in place, watching the pulsating light show; it was mesmerising, informing, educating and communicating!

Padrig was now clear on what he must do and he knew that Tanwen was not to be told. He would leave at first light the following morning.

*

"THEY ARE NEAR," said Lady Tanja.

# Chapter 11: Dämonen

"The Elven? How many are there?" said Queen Cartimandua.

"Only two, in fact the Council of Two."

"Council? What does that mean?"

"It's part of the governing structure of the Elven. They have a complex arrangement that uses their magic numbers. Two is one of those numbers. None of this is important at present but the Council of Two is their smallest unit and they don't risk it lightly."

"So, they are taking this seriously."

"As you would expect. But, two against the Dämonen seems foolhardy."

"It is as it is," said the Queen, "and what next for us?"

"We watch and wait until we know the whereabouts of the door and then we enter after them."

"That lacks sophistication," said the Queen, "how do we know that the door will remain open?"

"You must trust me," said Lady Tanja, "for I have powers that you cannot comprehend."

The Queen's face twisted at the slight but she said simply, "As you wish."

"There is another, faint and distant."

"What is the next Elven magic number?"

## Chapter 11: Dämonen

"IT IS NOT ELVEN."

Queen Cartimandua remained silent as she gathered her weapons, ready for the conquest to follow.

"YOU WILL NOT NEED THEM. THEY WILL BE OF NO USE IN DÄMONEN."

"I will not travel without them."

"IT IS A DRAGON. A MALE DRAGON, MOST UNUSUAL. I HAVE NOT SEEN HIS KIND IN A LONG TIME. WHAT CAN HE WANT?"

"What does that mean?" said the Queen.

*I am out of my depth.*

"NO, OH NO,"

Alarmed, Queen Cartimandua said, "What?"

"THE ELVEN, THEY HAVE INVOKED A CLOAKING SPELL. I CAN NO LONGER SEE THEM."

*

Padrig flew well above the two Elven figures that he'd spotted from far away; he was hoping that they would not see him. As the Elven descended he noticed a change; the two merged into a larger but less distinct entity.

*The Elven cloak. It doesn't fool dragons.*

He followed them down from a discrete distance, his keen vision watching the Elven, with grace, tumble from the sky. They were beautiful creatures and one of the Earth's finest.

# Chapter 11: Dämonen

High in the sky, Padrig circled, adjusting his head to keep his gaze fixed on their positions; this was easy for a dragon of Padrig's experience and years.

*

"Ah," said Lady Tanja.

The Queen remained silent.

"The dragon. He is not deceived by the Elven spell; he can see them yet. We must follow the dragon. It is time Queen. We will move quicker if you will allow me entry."

Queen Cartimandua swallowed and phlegm seemed to stick in her throat.

*I will never be ready for this.*

"If you must," she said.

"I need your compliance," said Lady Tanja, "or I may harm you. You must relax and make ready."

"So be it," said the Queen.

Queen Cartimandua perceived the chill as Lady Tanja merged into her id. It was not unpleasant and the Queen found that she could relax her defences. Soon, the Queen and Lady Tanja were one and Queen Cartimandua's personality hibernated; that of Lady Tanja dominated and the Queen felt a brief glimpse of the evil and awesome power of the Lady.

## Chapter 11: Dämonen

*It feels so good, so empowering, so nefarious.*

\*

The Council of Two of the Elven landed in a clearing with an ancient oak at its centre. Its branches extended strongly in all directions with the dominant boughs facing south; they created shadow beneath the tree and nothing grew in the oak's shade, nor at its boundary; magic was at work.

Tanyl, still respecting their pledge of silence, nodded to Ioelena who took an elaborately shaped piece of oak from her bag and placed it in an identically shaped orifice in the trunk of the tree. The outline of a door appeared in the colossal trunk and Ioelena pulled on the slot at it edge. It opened easily and the two Elven slipped inside. They closed the door behind them.

There was a weakness in their plan and they knew it. The door had but one key that opened it from outside; it could not be locked, from the inside. Those who constructed the door had never intended for it to be used again; it was to contain and never to allow exit. The smaller Elven Councils had argued for the destruction of the key but had been overruled by the Council of one hundred and twenty six. Tanyl and Ioelena relied on the integrity of the cloak spell and their oath of silence to protect their entry but they had not expected a dragon

# Chapter 11: Dämonen

to be watching them.

*

Padrig positioned himself above the Elven as they landed by the old oak tree. He watched with interest.

*They have entered the tree; that must be the door. Give them time, I do not wish to be seen.*

He touched down by the tree, manoeuvring himself through the forest canopy with ease. After examining the trunk of the oak he discovered the outline of the door and pulled it open.

*Too easy.*

He lowered his head, walked inside and pulled the door shut behind him. It closed with a soft clunk.

*

Lady Tanja watched the Dragon enter the door in the oak and smiled.

*I'm going home.*

# 12 – Labyrinth

The Elven cloaking spell was still operating as Ioelena and Tanyl passed through the door. It dissipated quickly; spells were of no use within the labyrinth. Inside the entrance was a small ledge and then the floor fell away revealing a dull red light below. They had memorised the map given to them by their elders; essential as it was forbidden for it to leave the Elven forest. Together they leapt from the sill into the void and flew down towards the welcoming glow; better than the dankness of the doorway, perhaps.

The descent was long and featureless; a well of dark grey granite with crystals sparkling to light their way. The floor beckoned; it seemed forever to be distant but gradually, with every wing flap, it came closer and more welcoming.

*Appearances can deceive.*

The Elven Council of Two knew what awaited them; they had seen the plan. At the pit bottom, entered through a duct, was a low vaulted cavern, hexagonal in structure and able to rotate about its centre. On one wall was a circular hole; an exit tube perfectly aligned with similar hexagonal cave and the start of the maze.

The labyrinth was formed by eight layers of interlocking

hexagonally shaped structures called nodes; each layer was below another and, at some points in the structure, hollow vertical shafts joined one layer to another. Manoeuvring through the maze required entry into a node, rotating it to align the exit tube of another node, moving to it and repeating the process until the shafts were found and all eight layers were negotiated to allow exit to Dämonen below.

*Some nodes house surprises; fatal surprises.*

Ioelena and Tanyl had practised incessantly and now it was real; the labyrinth permitted no mistakes. The Elven numbers, with a twist; the key to the labyrinth.

*The slant? The ancient Elven numbers included seven.*

2, **7**, 8, 20, 28, 50, 82, and 126: the number of secure nodes at each level and a clue to the number of turns needed to align it to its partner for the safe route through the network.

*Even this is may not be enough.*

They started manoeuvring the first layer; it had two safe nodes plus the one in which they were standing.

*Right one. Left two. Right six. Open the door.*

A tube to the next node was revealed and Ioelena and Tanyl walked through it towards the next node; the entry port closed behind them.

*No going back.*

# Chapter 12: Labyrinth

A door at the far end of the duct opened; they passed through it and it shut behind them. The node was empty.

*Repeat. Right eight. Left two. Open the door.*

Again, success. This time the exit was to the next layer through a hole in the floor. Like the other nodes, rotating allowed the opening to be aligned with the layer below.

*Right five.*

The layers were aligned perfectly. Ioelena and Tanyl descended to the next layer of the labyrinth. The node was empty.

*Success.*

*

Padrig arrived at the entry node of the labyrinth and reconnoitred his situation. He looked at the six sided cavern that he occupied and at the lever that was the only adornment. He had to squat for the node was not designed for his torso.

*Tanwen would not fit here; it's a squeeze for me too.*

There was a noise behind him and he turned awkwardly, his head rubbing against the ceiling. A figure alighted gently at the foot of the tunnel, the entrance to the labyrinth.

"Queen Cartimandua, I believe," said Padrig, "we have not met."

"INDEED WE HAVEN'T," said a voice that was not that of the

## Chapter 12: Labyrinth

Queen.

"Ah, the Queen is no more. You must be Malevolence incarnate, as it were."

"HALF CORRECT, MATE OF TANWEN, FIRE MANON, FOR QUEEN CARTIMANDUA IS LENDING ME HER BODY FOR OUR TRIP TO DÄMONEN BUT SHE IS SAFE. HERE, I AM LADY TANJA, TRUE AND ANCIENT RULER OF THE DÄMONEN AND ALL OF THE SHIRES OF YORK."

Padrig raised his head, difficult in the node, and his eyes pointed skywards.

*Tanwen would have flamed at this point; a show of her strength.*

"Padrig is my name." said Padrig, "The curse of the Dämonen, yes? You need a human in tow to cross to your homeland."

Lady Tanja ignored Padrig's judgement and entered the node to stand alongside him. Queen Cartimandua's shorter stature meant that she did not have to stoop and her head was well clear of the top of the cavern.

"Do you know how this works?" said Padrig.

"I SUGGEST THAT YOU LEAVE NOW FOR I AM NOT ENTERING DÄMONEN WITH A DRAGON."

"I am not leaving," said Padrig.

# Chapter 12: Labyrinth

"I THINK THAT YOU ARE," said Lady Tanja.

Padrig tumbled onto his side and slid from the node into the bottom of the entrance shaft. As he recovered his composure he watched Lady Tanja yank at the lever and the node turned, blocking his view. When the entrance drifted again into view, Lady Tanja was gone.

*Well, that went well.*

\*

Compared to the Elven, Lady Tanja should have been at a disadvantage, not having seen the plan of the labyrinth; she was aware that she was in a maze and found the prospect of navigating it alone daunting. Over the time of her exile she had learned many things, mostly from the mythology of humans; closely linked to fact but embellished by superstition.

*Mankind is a gullible species; it will believe the most unlikely of things.*

The Elven were different. The mortal enemy of the Dämonen and secretive; little of the knowledge they held escaped and the labyrinth's mystery was no exception.

*What is the probability of negotiating the labyrinth with success? Close to zero. That's the Elven assessment.*

They had miscalculated. Like a slug or snail leaves a trail betraying its path, so had the Elven and Lady Tanja could read it; all Dämonen could. She had to be quick for she could use this skill only in confined spaces like these and the trail would go cold quickly.

*With their cunning, do they not know this? Fools.*

Lady Tanja followed the scent trail left by the Council of Two. She manipulated the lever skilfully; her intention, two nodes behind the Elven.

*

Bruised by his encounter with Lady Tanja, Padrig picked himself up and brushed off the dust. He fluttered his wings in irritation.

*What would Tanwen have said? Defeated so easily.*

He re-entered the start node of the labyrinth, stooping so as not to hit his head on the roof. He looked at the lever and shrugged. He placed a claw on the clasp and pushed the mechanism forward. The node rotated about its centre until it came to a halt as Padrig released his grasp on the lever; it was arbitrary.

The node positioned itself so that the exit tube aligned itself with another node. Padrig heard the door slide open at the far end of the tube and then his own portal opened too.

A loud noise: scraping, scratching. It was coming his way.

A cloud of smoke followed by a flame of magnificent yellow

# Chapter 12: Labyrinth

rushed through from the far node.

It was unmistakable.

# 13 – Delyth

Dragons are immune to the effects of fire, otherwise Padrig would have been vaporised. The smoke and flame filled the chamber and surrounded Padrig who stood firm. There followed another blast, which irked him. He moved towards the tunnel, the source of the inferno and squeezed through, popping from the other end like a cork from a bottle.

The smoke cleared a little; enough to see what was causing the rumpus.

"You're a dragon," said a voice from within the cavern. This node was much larger than the one he'd come from.

"It can't be," said the voice, "no, it can't be."

Padrig blinked and his large lashes brushed the smoke from his eyes. His vision cleared. Before him stood a large female dragon and one that was much prettier than Tanwen.

"Delyth!" said Padrig.

"Padrig!" said Delyth.

*Delyth, an old flame of mine; well I never.*

"What are you doing here?" said Delyth.

"I could ask you the same thing," said Padrig.

Delyth stretched her wings and grinned. Padrig did the same.

"I searched for you," said Padrig, "I thought you'd left and

# Chapter 13: Delyth

didn't want to see me again."

"How could you think that," said Delyth and she moved closer so that she could rub Padrig's nose with her own.

Padrig was enjoying the sensation when a vision of Tanwen came into his mind. He stepped back, sharply.

"That was a long time ago, Delyth. I'm with Tanwen now."

"Tanwen?" said Delyth.

"You remember Tanwen. Quick to flame, short temper, red whiskers," said Padrig.

"Tanwen! What did you see in her and she was such a bossy beast."

*And still is!*

"We have two daughters," said Padrig, hoping to quash Delyth's ardour.

Delyth was disinterested in Padrig's domestic arrangements so she shifted tack.

"What are you doing here, Padrig?"

Padrig took a deep breath and explained to Delyth his quest to retrieve the crystals from Dämonen and return them to White Scar Cave.

"You know where you are don't you Padrig?" said Delyth.

"Yes, of course I do."

"Well, you are foolhardy," said Delyth, "nobody has ever

traversed the labyrinth and survived."

"I was following the Elven," said Padrig.

"Elven? They are here?" said Delyth.

"Yes, they are ahead of me, as is Lady Tanja in the body of Queen Cartimandua."

"Whoa, slow down," said Delyth, "just explain that, will you?"

Padrig explained and Delyth became more sombre as the story unfolded.

"Well, this is very serious I think," said Delyth, "thank goodness the second crystal is safe."

Padrig looked cagey and looked at the floor.

"You didn't, did you?"

Padrig fluttered his wings but continued to look down.

"That's just stupid Padrig, really dumb."

"It was agitated," said Padrig, "I couldn't leave it like that."

"Anyway," said Padrig, aiming to deflect the conversation away from him, "what are you doing here?"

"A good question! I've been trapped in here since you left me."

"I didn't leave," said Padrig.

"It seemed like that to me. Where were you when I needed you? Typical male."

# Chapter 13: Delyth

*She's beginning to sound like Tanwen.*

"Anyway, those Elven wanted someone to guard their precious labyrinth and they tricked me into agreeing."

*For a price I would think.*

"What I didn't know was that I would be cooped up in this cave. You are only the third creature to set foot in here and I'm sure you know what happened to the others?"

Padrig nodded sagely.

"I've had enough now," said Delyth, "I've done my duty, paid my dues. I'd like to see the outside again."

"Well, Delyth, there might be a problem there," said Padrig, "because you won't fit through that tunnel and you certainly will not fit in that chamber."

"Well, then," said Delyth, "you'd better keep me company."

Padrig heard the door from the labyrinth into the dragon's cave slam shut. His exit was now barred.

*

Lady Tanja was following the trail of the Elven.

*It's too fresh. They are too close.*

She wondered what was happening as she'd caught up with Ioelena and Tanyl. They were in the next node and they hadn't moved for a while.

*I don't want a confrontation. I will bide my time.*

# Chapter 13: Delyth

"Are you sure, Tanyl?" said Ioelena, "there can be no mistakes."

"Certain, I am not," Tanyl admitted, "but I am pretty sure. You?"

"Something seems to be different here. It isn't exactly the same as the plan."

"This is the last node," said Tanyl, "it would be a travesty to fail at this point."

"Yes," said Ioelena, "but wait Tanyl. I would like to go through it with you."

"Right."

"We are at the lowest level, the eighth, yes?" said Ioelena, continuing without waiting for Tanyl to answer, "but in Elven mythology there are only seven levels."

"The seven magic numbers," said Tanyl.

"We have been following the ancients scheme. But I think that is the twist. The exit to the maze is on level seven, not eight. Seven is the number of the witch, is it not?" said Ioelena.

"I see where you are going," said Tanyl, "witches and the devil. Smart."

"Am I right?" said Ioelena, "We can afford no blunders."

Tanyl took a moment to consider what Ioelena had told him.

# Chapter 13: Delyth

He tried to put himself in the mind of the labyrinth designer but that was too difficult.

*We have to go with our instincts and pay for the consequences, with our lives if it is required.*

"Let us do it," Tanyl said, finally, "I am sure."

"It will mean retracing our steps for the last three nodes so that we can fly up to level seven," said Ioelena.

They turned back and the door to the prior node slid open to reveal Lady Tanja, in the guise of Queen Cartimandua, standing at the centre of the node.

*

"How did you get in here?" said Padrig, "Did they build this around you?"

"It's a long time ago Padrig," said Delyth, "but this cave is an ancient one. It's been here long before the labyrinth."

"So, they did build the labyrinth around the cave?"

"No, I came in here myself."

Padrig was starting to become exasperated.

"How?" he said.

"Well, I flew in of course," said Delyth.

"From where?" said Padrig and he sighed.

"Up there," Delyth said and pointed with her claw, "but they filled in the hole."

# Chapter 13: Delyth

"Let me take a look," said Padrig, "but just tell me exactly where the exit was."

Delyth came close to Padrig and he smelt the beautiful aroma of fresh smoke. He followed the line of her outstretched claw to a craggy section of rock high in the roof.

"Just there, Padrig," Delyth said.

He opened his wings and flapped them gently until he started to rise. Then he created a down draught using his strong muscles and rose towards the top of the cave. He reached the ridge and looked at the work of the Elven.

*They haven't used magic. I wonder why?*

The exit had been closed conventionally using smaller rocks. Over the years the mortar had crumbled and some of the stones were loose.

*Hasn't she tried to free herself? Tanwen would have been out of here in minutes.*

Padrig pulled at some of the looser rocks and they came away easily, tumbling to the floor far below. He watched as Delyth scrambled out of the way. He used his strength to slacken some more; they were soon free and falling. Then he found the key rocks and a large section of the ceiling came away and tumbled to the foot of the cave, generating a cloud of dust. Above Padrig was a hollow circular shaft, wide enough

# Chapter 13: Delyth

for a female dragon, and a circle of light far above.

*

"Queen Cartimandua," said Ioelena, "an unexpected pleasure but, wait, you are not what you seem."

"You feel it too," said Tanyl.

"Malevolence, if I am not mistaken. This is different though, for I can still sense you Queen, though your are sleeping," said Ioelena.

"We can not allow this," said Tanyl, "and your powers are useless in the labyrinth."

"AS ARE YOURS TOO," said Lady Tanja.

*They do not know who I am.*

"Why are you here Malevolence?" said Ioelena, "Your guidance was that the Elven were to recover the crystals from Dämonen. You made no mention that you wished to accompany us. It is forbidden in any case. And how did you make it this far through the labyrinth. I smell treachery."

"She is following us," said Tanyl.

"Is that so?" said Ioelena, "Speak."

*What do I do now?*

"I WANTED TO BE SURE THAT YOU WOULD COMPLETE THE MISSION," said Lady Tanja.

"How did you reach so far into the labyrinth?" said Tanyl.

# Chapter 13: Delyth

"I think it best that you tell us," said Ioelena.

"OR YOU DO WHAT?" said Lady Tanja, "WE BOTH HAVE LIMITED POWERS HERE."

A stand-off was developing; Lady Tanja was watching her route to Dämonen disappearing.

*I have to do something.*

"IS IT NOT POSSIBLE FOR US TO DO THIS TOGETHER? I AM AN APPARITION, AFTER ALL. I NEEDED THE DEAR QUEEN'S BODY TO COME THIS FAR."

Ioelena and Tanyl spoke in the ancient Elven tongue, hoping that Lady Tanja would not understand and they were correct; she could not speak ancient Elven.

"This is very irregular," said Tanyl, "but what choice do we have? We leave her here? If we do she will follow us again. Take her back? We risk all that we have achieved."

"What would our elders do?" said Ioelena.

"They are not here to advise," said Tanyl, "and I know that our culture is inclusive, consultative, but we are here, alone, and we must make the decision as a Council of Two. What is your decision Ioelena?"

Ioelena was tormented with doubt. Slowly, she made her choice.

"We take her," said Ioelena.

# Chapter 13: Delyth

"Agreed," said Tanyl.

"But we record that this is a decision forced upon us by circumstances," said Ioelena.

"Yes," said Tanyl, "let it be so."

They switched back to the familiar tongue and Ioelena spoke first.

"You will come with us."

*

"Come Delyth, what is stopping you?" said Padrig.

Delyth was dragging her feet; she didn't seem to want to leave the cave.

"It's the shackles," she said, "I can't fly."

"What shackles?" said Padrig.

*What's wrong with her?*

"Around my feet," said Delyth, "an Elf put them on. They are magic. I can't leave here until they are removed."

"There are no chains around your feet Delyth," said Padrig, "honestly."

"You just can't see them, but they're there."

Padrig checked around Delyth's feet to feel for manacles. He could feel none.

*It explains it, why she hadn't tried to escape.*

"Believe me Delyth, you have no shackles around your feet,

magic or otherwise. Come on, try to move. Walk if you don't want to fly."

Delyth was reluctant.

"Look, girl, you've been tricked. Magic doesn't seem to work in the labyrinth in any case. Elven power can't be used in here. Really," said Padrig.

*I sound desperate. Calm down Padrig, give her space.*

Delyth took a tentative step. Then another and another.

*So far, so good.*

She was at the far side of the cavern and Padrig shouted over to her.

"Can you feel any chains?"

"Well, now you come to mention it," said Delyth, "no."

"Do you want to try and fly, slowly at first if you like?" said Padrig.

Delyth gave a grimace and Padrig encouraged her to continue. She flapped her large strong wings gently at first and Padrig felt the breeze of air pushed aside by her exertions. Delyth increased the power of each stroke and her enormous body lurched upwards. Tentative at first, Delyth circled the space above Padrig's head.

*No manacles.*

She pushed her wings down and Delyth soared upwards

towards the opening in the roof. There was no turning back; she made for the exit and Padrig took to the air to follow her. She had a lead on him and he had to flap his wings furiously to catch up with her. As Padrig came close he spotted the wide grin on Delyth's face and whispers of grey smoke emerging from her nostrils.

*Does it get better than this?*

They flew into the open air through the egress and into a place that was not a Thriding of the Shires of York.

*

Ioelena and Tanyl were standing, with their unexpected companion, in the final node of the labyrinth at level seven.

"This is it," said Ioelena.

"Yes, are you ready?" said Tanyl.

"Malevolence, we are about to enter Dämonen and things may become dangerous; we are not sure what will happen next."

"YOU ARE NOT SURE?"

"We have been following our plan, up to now," said Tanyl, "but Dämonen is controlled by others and not the Elven. We expect to exit the maze in the Crystal Chamber and we calculate it to be empty. But, we are not wholly confident and we have no way of knowing."

# Chapter 13: Delyth

"I SEE," said Lady Tanja.

*I'm indifferent. Once inside Dämonen things will improve for me, significantly.*

"Let us continue," said Ioelena, "Seven, yes?"

Tanyl nodded and they turned the node through seven notches to the right. The exit lined up precisely with the tunnel and the door at the far end opened.

Silence.

"As we have agreed, Ioelena, you must stay and keep the labyrinth open for our return" said Tanyl and he left the node.

Ioelena remained. Lady Tanja waited for a moment and then continued after Tanyl. The plan had been on target and Tanyl stepped into a cavern and gazed upon the podium that housed the Crystal Chamber. On top of the podium was the third crystal.

*Of course, it can't be placed into the chamber without the second.*

His senses were alert.

*Something isn't right but I don't know what.*

Lady Tanja stepped into Dämonen and the face of Queen Cartimandua smiled before her body dropped to the floor and groaned. Lady Tanja emerged from the Queen and the form of a devil materialised in front of the Elf.

# Chapter 13: Delyth

"I am home," said Lady Tanja and she stretched out her wings, "and I have a score to settle."

Tanyl gasped loudly, causing Ioelena to rush from the labyrinth. The door closed behind her.

# 14 – Dämonen

Padrig looked around at the high mountain peaks and at a sky that didn't look right.

*It's too perfect.*

"This isn't the Shires," he said and his words were blown away with the breeze.

Delyth beckoned to a nearby summit where there was a ledge. She landed deftly on it and Padrig followed her.

"Where are we?" Delyth said, "we're not in the Shires, are we?"

Padrig looked around. It was a mountainous country littered with great peaks.

*It has a stark beauty but it seems so barren.*

"It must be Dämonen." said Padrig, "for where else could we be?"

"A flaw in the Elven plan," said Delyth.

"What?" said Padrig.

"Well, if this is Dämonen, and I think you must be right, then there's a way in without going through the labyrinth."

Padrig deliberated for a moment.

"Guarded by you Delyth," he said, "and a set of non-existent magic manacles."

# Chapter 14: Dämonen

Delyth chuckled and said, "Ironic isn't it? I could have freed myself any time I'd wanted."

"But no way back, for you at least," said Padrig, solemnly.

"How so?" said Delyth.

"Remember the way in? It's too small for you, and you can't negotiate the labyrinth. It's made for the Elven, not for our kind," said Padrig.

A tear dribbled down Delyth's cheek and hissed as it reached her nostril, evaporating in the heat and leaving a white salty mark.

"We'll find a way," said Padrig, trying to reassure.

*Though I don't know how right now.*

Padrig looked down from the sill at the precipitous drop. He wondered how the ledge came to be there; it looked manufactured. An answer came more quickly than he'd anticipated when the section of rock behind him opened and a startled Albert was confronted by a couple of dragons resting on his ledge.

A surprised Delyth flew off the ledge first with Padrig in hot pursuit. They ascended so that they could look down on Albert, now balanced on the rim. He was smaller than Padrig and Padrig could see scaly skin, leathery wings, horns on the top of his head and a broad, pointed tail.

## Chapter 14: Dämonen

*The mythology is right; the Dämonen are devils.*

Delyth and Padrig circled in close formation.

"We are in Dämonen," said Padrig, "that is one of them."

"It looks like it can fly," said Delyth.

"Yes, but he's small, even smaller than me," said Padrig.

"I've heard they have huge powers, Padrig. I'm scared," said Delyth.

"So have you," said Padrig, alarmed by Delyth's lack of self confidence.

*If only Tanwen was here.*

\*

Albert was on his way to visit Lord Alaric when he encountered Padrig and Delyth resting on his perch. They had surprised him but he had little time for them; Lord Alaric was very insistent.

*I must go now.*

He watched the dragons circling above him before he leapt from the ledge and flew towards the great hall. The dragons did not follow.

*I'll have to deal with them later.*

His encounter had disturbed him and he remembered little of the flight between the Kapell and Lord Alaric's residence so his arrival seemed sooner than he'd anticipated. He'd had little

# Chapter 14: Dämonen

time to prepare for the Lord of Dämonen.

Albert shuffled into the hall and the greeting ritual was fulfilled briskly. Lord Alaric looked agitated; unusual as he was normally composure personified.

"Lord, I came as quickly as I could."

"Albert," said Lord Alaric.

*This is serious. He's calling me Albert already.*

Albert sniffed and looked around.

*Just Alaric and myself. No von Brunhild.*

"Albert," said Lord Alaric, trying to retain his dignity but Albert could see that something had spooked him, "I have had a message."

"A message, Lord," said Albert.

"Yes, Albert," said Alaric, "delivered by Alder."

Albert waited.

*Silence is such a useful instrument.*

"From Lady Tanja," said Lord Alaric.

Albert's eyebrows twitched and he said, "What does it say?"

"It says," said Alaric, tersely, "that she is here, in Dämonen."

Albert was silent again.

"How can this be? How is it that you and von Brunhild were not aware of this?"

"She is difficult to track," said Albert.

## Chapter 14: Dämonen

*That is so weak.*

"We do know that we have not always been able to trace her in the Shires," said Albert.

"So said von Brunhild too," said Alaric.

"Look, Albert, this is very serious. I am relying upon you to find and remove the Lady, and quickly."

*The implication is obvious; he wants me, not von Brunhild, to sort out this problem.*

"Yes, Lord, Immediately."

He left the hall rapidly and his mind was fomenting; thoughts of dragons in Dämonen were receding.

*Time to decide, Albert. Who's side are you on?*

The winner of the contest for supreme power would most likely be decided by the answer to Albert's question and it came quickly to him.

*

Ioelena knelt before Queen Cartimandua, who was lying prone on the floor. The Queen was weak and her time was short. She signalled for Ioelena to come closer and the small Elf obliged.

"Do not trust them," whispered the Queen, "they have no soul; I have seen. Take heed. Grave peril awaits us all."

Ioelena watched as the Queen's body faded and melted into

the surroundings. Soon the Queen was gone.

*Is that the Dämonen way of handling the end of a mortal?*

Lady Tanja looked on but was disinterested. She had what she wanted.

"I see you have forfeited your path from Dämonen. That was audacious. I have no need for you and I have no wish to expend my energy on the Elven. I have sealed the entrance to this chamber; there is no one in Dämonen powerful enough to release it."

"Are we trapped here?" said Tanyl.

"I have no wish for your presence any longer than is necessary. In any other circumstances you and your kind would be my adversary. You are of no consequence to me now. I will release the exit into the tunnel that leads through the mountain into the Valley of the Veils."

"And then what?" said Ioelena.

"I care not," said Lady Tanja, "take it or leave it."

"We take it," said Tanyl, "for we have no wish to spend any further time with your kind."

"Watch your tongue little Elf," said Lady Tanja, "my power remains to be tested since I returned. Do not tempt me further."

Tanyl looked at Ioelena who was urging caution.

"Come," said Lady Tanja.

# Chapter 14: Dämonen

She led them to the rear of the Crystal Chamber into a tunnel closed at its far end. The Lady placed her hand against the rock face and it dissolved to reveal a room hewn into the rock with an exit tube directly opposite. She urged the Elven forward and they entered the room and looked around.

Their entry point was resealed and they were alone in the room.

*

Delyth flew high into the sky and Padrig followed her. Gliding in the breeze they stayed together so that they could talk.

"It is so mountainous," said Delyth, "I am not sure how this can all be like this. We are underground, are we not?"

"A land of strangeness," said Padrig, "but never forget the capability of the Dämonen. They have been contained by the Elven for so many aeons. I fear that we are entering a new age, an age of darkness."

"You are frightening me Padrig. Come, let us find some food, I am hungry."

Far in the distance Delyth could see dark grey smoke and ash emerging from a large area glowing a deep orange red and reflecting upwards. These were the Magma Mort, a vast cauldron of seething liquid rock. She looked away.

## Chapter 14: Dämonen

*This land is so inhospitable.*

This was to change as Padrig gazed around and his keen sight spotted a rare fertile valley, covered in trees under the artificial blue grey sky.

"Over there," he said, "the valley, can you see it."

"Of course I can," said Delyth, "and it is so welcome."

"Let's see if we can find anything there. There must be something to eat in the lowland; even the Dämonen have to eat, don't they?"

Padrig led the way and, as he flew, he could hear the gentle pad of Delyth's wings.

*A mesmerising sound.*

As they closed on the vale, Padrig shouted to Delyth.

"There aren't many valleys, Delyth. Strange land. Did you see the deer?"

"Yes. Food," said Delyth, succinctly.

After a meal of dragon roast venison they explored their surroundings. It was an Eden and life was abundant with all manner of flora and fauna; a stark contrast to the rest of Dämonen. Flying low over the valley the dragons spotted a path leading from the mountain into a wood and exiting in a large clearing surrounded by ancient trees.

"Down there," said Padrig, "let's take a look."

# Chapter 14: Dämonen

They landed at the centre of the glade onto soft green meadow speckled with flowers in eternal bloom.

*Truly an Eden?*

Arranged evenly around the edge of the clearing were four arches, each held in place by columns of dressed stone. The arches were a dragon's height and width. Large enough to allow the passage of a female dragon through the arch and spacious for Padrig.

*Yet the arch leads to and from nowhere.*

"The stone is so beautifully cut,"said Delyth.

"The work of Elven hands, I think," said Padrig, "for there is no other creature who could manufacture so finely."

Engrossed, Padrig and Delyth failed to notice the arrival of two diminutive figures as they touched down behind them.

"The work is indeed Elven," said Tanyl, "and it is more beautiful than even I had imagined."

Padrig turned, alarmed at the intrusion and a small flame erupted from Delyth's mouth, expressing her tension.

"Ah, it is you," said Padrig.

"You know these Elven, Padrig. You mix with strange folk," said Delyth.

"And it is you also," said Ioelena, "I will not ask how you arrived here but I am grateful that you are. But, you have the

# Chapter 14: Dämonen

second crystal, do you not? I ask, is this wise?"

*They think that Delyth is Tanwen.*

"I had missed that, Ioelena," said Tanyl.

"Yes," said Delyth, "foolish in my view. Are you going to introduce me?"

"I know them only through Tanwen," said Padrig, "but, if I am not mistaken, this is the Elven Council of Two. Am I correct?"

"Yes, and this is Tanwen, Fire Manon of the Dragons?" said Ioelena.

"Indeed I am not, Elf," said Delyth, "I am Delyth."

"Guardian of the labyrinth," said Tanyl, "I think I see."

"I am Padrig, mate of Tanwen and I will explain."

Padrig explained to the Elven what he knew and, when he'd finished, said, "I don't know where we are and hope that you can enlighten us."

Ioelena looked at Tanyl and he nodded.

"You are in the Valley of the Veils of the Shires of York. The veils, as you surmised, are of Elven construction and allow passage between Dämonen and the Shires. They are activated by the Crystals of the Veil and three crystals are needed for each veil. But you know that Padrig, for your kind were chosen to attend to the crystals and keep them safe."

## Chapter 14: Dämonen

Padrig acknowledged by fluttering his wings and Ioelena continued.

"Our only way back to the Shires now is through a veil but we cannot allow the final crystal to come into the possession of the Dämonen."

"Or the age of darkness really does begin," said Padrig.

"Yes," said Tanyl.

# 15 – Rift

Albert looked out over Dämonen from the ledge outside the Kapell. He stood there when he needed time to think and it was such a time. On this occasion he would be interrupted as the High Priest Eburwin opened the door from the other side and motioned for Albert to enter. Inside were the other High Priest, Gervas, and a surprise: Baron von Brunhild.

Albert entered and said, "Baron, we do not often see you here."

*We never see you here.*

"Come, Albert," said the Baron, "we must set aside our differences for once."

*He called me Albert. Extraordinary!*

"I know why you are all here," said Albert, "and little else has occupied my thoughts. The rift in our leadership: Alaric and Tanja."

"Yes," said Eburwin, "you are correct."

"I think we both know where Lady Tanja is," said the Baron.

Albert raised his eyebrows and fluttered his wings. It was unusual for Baron von Brunhild to share intelligence.

"She has bunkered down within the Crystal Chamber complex and, as you know, it is vast with few exits," said von

## Chapter 15: Rift

Brunhild.

"But one to the valley," said Gervas.

"The Lady Tanja has sealed these exits," said the Baron, "and you know that she possesses exceptional skills, shall we call them, to rival those of Lord Alaric."

"I know that we are both watching these exits," said Albert.

"Exactly," said the Baron, "but let me not prevaricate. I think it is time we worked differently."

"Differently?" said Albert.

*I still don't trust him.*

"High Priests," said Baron von Brunhild, addressing them all, "the Lord of Dämonen ensures that we are continually in conflict. He says that it sharpens us; we compete for his attention."

Albert looked at his High Priests. They were listening emphatically. Von Brunhild continued.

"The arrival of the Lady Tanja changes everything. You must have noticed, Albert, that the Lord is distracted."

*He is. Vulnerable.*

"The balance within Dämonen is changing and old alliances are drifting. You are too good at your tasks High Priests to not know this. If we allow it to continue we will have another power struggle that will last a millennium; our land will be torn apart again and at a time when our goal is close at hand."

*He knows?*

"Our goal?" said Albert.

"Don't pretend," said the Baron and his wings fluttered with annoyance, "I am here to propose a new era of collaboration between us. Do not trifle with me, Albert."

"You know too," said Albert.

"The crystal," said the Baron, figuratively dancing around Albert.

*He knows.*

"It is here, in Dämonen," said Albert.

"In the valley. A dragon has it. I have held off retrieving it until we met. I know that you have only just discovered this too."

Albert was uncomfortable for this level of accord between them was without precedent.

"What is it you are proposing, Baron?"

"The end of tyranny," said the von Brunhild, "We have a choice. We support Alaric against Tanja or the other way round, I care not. Whoever wins will create their own form of personality cult; we see it now and it was like this in the past."

"I'm not sure I understand," said Gervas.

Albert was less puzzled.

## Chapter 15: Rift

"I am suggesting," said the Baron, "that we support neither and we used our combined forces to spawn a new order."

"A new order?" said Eburwin, "How will that help?"

"Yes," said Albert, interested, "what kind of order?"

"Are you able to imagine," said von Brunhild, "leadership based upon consensus with a senate of leaders, chosen for their abilities, working together for the good of all?"

"Sounds unworkable," said Gervas, "and not the Dämonen way."

"Let him finish," said Albert, "for our way has led to isolation from our rightful place in the Shires of York and defeat by the Elven."

"You make my point eloquently, High Priest," said the Baron, "for the Elven operate collaboratively. It is their strength for they do not follow a leader slavishly as we do, whatever their direction and capability. Inferior to us the Elven may be, but they have contained us for aeons. It is time to take our place in the Shires and we must not underestimate them this time."

"If my understanding is correct, Baron, I think you are proposing the end of the rule of both Lord Alaric and Lady Tanja?" said Albert.

"Yes, and I am sure you know what that means," said von

# Chapter 15: Rift

Brunhild.

"Indeed I do," said Albert and he looked at his fellow high priests.

"Treason?" said Gervas.

"Against whom?" said Albert, "Alaric or Tanja. Only one has a legitimate claim to the throne. Lord Alaric achieved his crown by conflict; he appointed himself."

"It is time to choose," said the Baron, "continue with these power games and destroy Dämonen or rise above them and create a land of conquest and restore our position within the Shires."

"You know that if we agree," said Albert, "that we must do what Alaric failed to do for Lady Tanja."

Eburwin looked at Albert and then at Gervas.

"Their permanent destruction, Alaric and Tanja," he said, "so that they cannot return."

"Yes," said the Baron, "the Magma Mort. The only option open to us."

Albert was uneasy.

*

Lady Tanja was not wasting her time. Memories in Dämonen were long and she still had many followers. She used her powers to make contact and judged that over half of

# Chapter 15: Rift

Dämonen supported her.

*It is enough.*

She knew that she could achieve little from her sanctuary in the crystal chamber and that she had to set up a campaign headquarters and muster her troops around her. She chose the Magma Stasis, south of the Magma Mort, where the original Dämonen court was located. Lady Tanja summoned her faithful supporters and made for her base within Dämonen.

*Let the conflict begin Lord Alaric. There will be no mercy and I will take what is rightfully mine.*

*

"Have you seen it?" said Padrig.

"In the sky?" said Delyth.

"What do you mean?" said Tanyl.

"Look," said Padrig, pointing to the west.

"Come, fly with us," said Delyth and she flapped her wings.

They took off and circled the Valley of the Veils. To the west, heading for the ancient citadel, was what looked like a dark swarm of tens of thousands of individuals. The formation seemed endless and they watched as those at the head descended into the stronghold at Magma Stasis like starlings on an autumn night.

"What's happening?" said Delyth.

# Chapter 15: Rift

"I don't know," said Padrig.

"Lady Tanja," said Ioelena, shouting to be heard, "she has called her supporters to her and has taken up residence in the old Dämonen capital."

"But how?" said Padrig, "The Lady has not ruled Dämonen for a long time."

"Time is different in Dämonen," said Tanyl, "and they live on a different scale to mortals."

"She still has followers?" said Delyth.

"Yes," said Ioelena, "as you can see. This marks the start of a time of great strife within Dämonen. We need to escape or we will be caught up in it."

"How do you suggest that we do that?" said Delyth.

"Padrig, the solution is with you. You have the second crystal. We need to return to the crystal chamber and open the passage through the Veil of Mowbray.

"I cannot do that," said Padrig, "I am the custodian of the crystals and I cannot let them fall into Dämonen hands."

Tanyl was about to speak when Padrig was accosted from behind. Neither the dragons nor Elven had noticed the arrival of the High Priest Guards; they singled out Padrig for they knew that he had the crystal. Surprised by the attack, Padrig tumbled from the sky. Delyth was quick to act and dropped so

## Chapter 15: Rift

that she was below Padrig to cushion his fall. He stopped before meeting Delyth and was side swiped by two of the Dämonen guards.

"Catch this," said Padrig and passed to her the crystal from under his wing.

She caught it easily and veered off to her left. The guards followed and Padrig swooped underneath her. As the guards closed in on Delyth she dropped the crystal and Padrig grasped it from the air. He flapped his wings furiously and rose into the air but hadn't noticed the guard above him who swooped towards Padrig and grasped the crystal. Delyth lurched towards the guard but she wasn't quick enough and he flew rapidly back towards the grand hall of Dämonen. Delyth tried to pursue them but they were too fast so she turned back.

Tanyl and Ioelena had landed already when Padrig touched down by the stone arches in the Valley of the Veils. Delyth descended later and she and Padrig rubbed noses in greeting.

"I'm sorry Padrig," said Delyth, "they were too quick for me."

"You did your best," said Padrig, "and for a moment I thought we had them."

"It was not to be," said Ioelena, "but they have the second crystal now. They were heading towards the great hall and Lord

## Chapter 15: Rift

Alaric so they must have been Alaric's defenders."

"No," said Tanyl, "they were High Priest guards and they were heading for the Kapell and not the great hall."

"Is that pertinent at all?" said Delyth.

"It may be," said Tanyl, "for it is rare for the High Priest guard to leave the Kapell; their role is solely to protect the High Priesthood of Dämonen."

*

Some hours later Padrig heard a loud humming sound and a sheen appeared within the first of the arches.

*It is beautiful; like water but less tangible and the blue sheen is alluring.*

Tanyl heard it too and walked over to where Padrig was standing.

"It is time," said Tanyl.

"To return?" said Padrig.

"Yes," said Tanyl, "they have activated the Veil of Mowbray and we have a way back."

"And, so do they," said Delyth.

"It is true," said Ioelena, as she joined them by the stone arch.

"Come," said Tanyl and he held Ioelena's hand as they walked through the centre of the arch and disappeared.

# Chapter 15: Rift

"Goodbye to you too," said Padrig, "We had better go single file. After you Delyth. I'll be right along."

Gingerly, keeping to the middle, Delyth stepped through the arch to materialise in a valley of the Shires of York.

Padrig looked back, taking a last look at the peaks of Dämonen, causing him to trip and hit the vertical column of the arch. He stumbled through to his homeland and safety, or so he thought.

# A Final Word

The next book in this series "The Shires of York – Two: Turmoil" is now available.

It follows on from this book and chronicles the troubles brewed in Dämonen and its attempt to move from totalitarian rule to one that is more collaborative, maybe.

The mortal Shires of York moves on a different time frame to that of Dämonen and the Shires meet their next challenge: the invasion of the Vikings from the Norse countries.

The first Veil of York into Mowbray brings new challenges for the Shires whilst Dämonen is preoccupied with its power struggles. Some in Dämonen see the veil as bringing new opportunities and are intent on grasping them.

**If you enjoyed the book then please leave a review; if you didn't please tell me why and I'll try harder.**

You can contact me through Wise Grey Owl.

21668476R00101

Printed in Great Britain
by Amazon